POST-TERRA FIRMA

THE FAMILY

SAXON KEELEY

Also by Saxon Keeley

Some Velvet Morning
Blue Light

For Danny,

   Thank you for my education in the deepest and darkest recesses of all things 'nerd'. Without it, I fear life would be taken too seriously and I may have succumbed to the mundane routine of everydayness. Heaven forbid!

POST-TERRA FIRMA

THE FAMILY

POST-TERRA FIRMA

RESONANCE

THE FAMILY

RESONANCE

FROM THE DUST

Jotunhiem

The dust is dry. It is swept up by the blustering winds. Inhaling it irritates the back of the throat. Coughing, the lone figure hocks up a combination of dirt and phlegm. Unfazed by the unpleasant mixture residing in his mouth, he waits for the wind to settle before he spits it out onto the ground.

Refusing to take another breath until he is certain he won't get another mouthful, he zips up his long, black coat, which reaches from just above his knees all the way up to the ridge of his nose. The high collar is tight enough around his face to ensure most of the dirt does not fall through the gaps. The material is tough, protecting his body from the elements.

As another gust of wind howls, more dust is blown into air. In the middle of a thick grey cloud, he uses his arm to shield his face. Squinting, his eyes are open just enough to still see the dim sun light shining through.

Subsiding once again, the lone man looks out into the distance. Along the horizon emerges a small settlement. Low in stature, but large enough to call it a town.

Jotunhiem is littered with small mining colonies. Each isolated from one another. Despite colonies spread throughout the Charted Systems, life on the Outer-Core colonies is pretty much the same wherever. Neighbouring town's folk are foreign enough for those living on planets such as this. Prospects of ordinary people are defined by a crude economic structure. There are plenty who are unfortunate enough to be born on the wrong rock. Either the planet's soil is rich in nutrients and the climate is mild enough, so the land is used to farm, or if the soil fails to

1

grow crops, then it is used to mine natural resources. Nothing could ever grow on the barren earth of Jotunhiem. It scarcely rains. This is not a land of plenty. It is a cog in a much larger and systematic machine, under the control of the Loyalists. So long as they provide metals, the Loyalist governments will provide them with water and food.

The man wanders into the outskirts of the town. Amongst the grey, characterless buildings, an almost silent humming can be heard from underfoot. Just below the ground are machines busy at work, separating and cleaning the ore from the mines.

Children play in the dust that has been swept into town. Women and men wrap scrap cloth and scarfs around their faces for protection. Compared to their rags, the lone wanderer seems well dressed. Something alien to the base needs of the colonists. Every one of them has a well-built physique, muscle carved from a lifetime of work in the mines. A sooty grime covers them, as if it were a proud second skin.

Walking further into the centre of town, more people stop what they are doing to stare at the stranger.

Momentarily the planet is shrouded in darkness as one of Jotunhiem's moons eclipses the sun. Everything grey disappears. The white of the miner's eyes shine through the dark. Not concerned by the attention he is drawing; the man looks around for someone to ask for directions. Under a makeshift porch, an old man on the verge of sleeping rocks back and forth on his chair.

"*Ni hao*," said the wanderer perfectly.

"No one out here speaks none of that Chinese son. Relax, just say 'Hello' for heaven's sake," interrupted the old miner.

The wrinkles of the old man are deep. His hands grip to the arms of his rocking chair, but are stiff and numb, lacking any real strength.

"Hello," replied the stranger.

"That's better," said the old man with a smile across his face. "What can I do for you?"

"I think I'm lost…"

"Lost? Ain't any wonder, dressed like that. Don't tell, me you came in from the dust? No one coming in from the dust is ever good news," explained the old miner.

The stranger smiles from behind his coat.

"I'm supposed to be meeting someone. They said to head to The Cackler. Not even sure if I'm on the right side of the planet," he admitted.

The people closely watch the interaction with the stranger.

The old man chuckles. "Well, you're in the right place. Down the block, and head right. You'll end up on Main Street, or what we call Main Street. Just behind the Supply Station, you can't miss it."

"Thanks," said the stranger, then walks off down the street.

"Now don't be causing no trouble, you hear?" called out the old man before he is completely out of earshot.

Either the words of warning were lost to the wind or fell on deaf ears.

Just as the old man said, *down on Main Street and behind the Supply Station. You can't miss it.* The stranger looks at the makeshift sign hanging above the entrance. Rusted scrap metal that has been lovingly crafted. Back lit, a dull light barely penetrates through the grey of the planet, unlike the smell of cheap stale alcohol.

3

Excitement and hesitation washes over the wandering man. A moment of lost composure overwhelms his thoughts. He holds his hand out towards the door handle. He breaths in a deeply. Holds his breath for five seconds and exhales slowly. Again, another five seconds.

"One drink, until he gets here," he muttered to himself under his breath.

With that he pushes open the door and quickly closes the it behind him so to keep out the dust. As he unzips his coat he notices the bar has fallen quiet. The men and women of the bar all turn to check out the stranger.

Behind the bar stands the owner and a waitress. The owner looks as well built as any of the miners, but the definition of his muscle is different. Less mass around his arms, instead his build is more evenly dispersed. Burns and scars scatter the owners skin. On his right arm is a tattoo of an old insignia from the war. Though the stranger cannot place the exact regiment of the insignia, he knows it did not belong to the same side he once fought for.

To break the tension in the bar, the owner nudges the waitress with his elbow, gently pushing her towards the bar.

"Hey ya, what you are having?" called out the waitress.

She is young, clean skin, hair that glows, physically dainty, but she has the same strong Scandinavian features as the rest of the people of the colony.

Her nails are clean, notices the stranger as he approaches the bar and takes a seat on one of the stools. Her perfume is sweet, floral and cheap. Her smile puts her out of place. It doesn't seem like she's ever done a hard day's work in her life, unlike the rest of the colonists.

"I'll have a scotch," he said while nodding to what looks to be the fullest and most expensive bottle on the shelf, pleasantly surprised to see a drink like that in a place such as this.

"Er...You sure about that Mr?" she questioned, looking back behind her at the bottle she has never once poured a glass of. "Shall I check the price for you? It could be quite expensive."

The stranger reaches into his trouser pocket and pulls out a real brown leather wallet. She watches bemused at the sight of the authentic material. Out from the wallet he finds out an emerald card. The card glimmers in the light of the bar. On each side is the Chinese symbol for *'family'*.

"I'm sure this will cover it," he smiled arrogantly.

"Oh," remarked the waitress, not quite sure what the card is, questioning if she should be wary of the stranger or comforted.

Once the payment is taken, she hands back the card and lays out a glass in front of him. The smell of a smoky whiskey hits the stranger's nostrils. The waitress is generous on the serving. Just as he puts the glass to his lips, someone takes a seat on the stool next to him.

"Hey Freya, can I get another one. Cheers doll," demanded the miner in a raspy voice.

The stranger sips his drink, ignoring the presence of the man sitting next to him.

"You know," said the miner to the stranger, "you look familiar. Don't I know you?"

The stranger takes a second from his drink and looks the miner up and down. He then looks him straight in the eye, indifferently he turns back forwards.

"I think your mistaken. Never met you in my life."

"Nah, nah," protested the miner, "I know you. I've seen your face somewhere before. Where have I seen you before?"

He begins scratching his cheek. The bristles of his stubble being ran over by the rough skin of his fingers make the sound of a match being slowly struck. Flecks of dry skin sprinkle the bar. Then, in a moment of clarity his face lights up. He leans in closer to the stranger, a waft of sour ale following him. Physically repulsed, the wanderer tips his head away and straightens up to the drunk miner.

"I knew I recognised you. You're that big hero guy? Aren't you," the miner said with a bitter resentment in his voice. "You're Daniel Hayward."

Daniel nods to himself, before turning back to his drink.

"I think you have the wrong guy. That ain't me," said Daniel.

The miner places a hand on Daniel's shoulder, holding him in place.

"Yeah, that's you. You killed a lot of people in the war. They called you a hero. Your face was all over the news when Nibiru fell. You've got one of those faces…hard to forget. I don't know, maybe it's because you killed a lot of people that day. I don't think there is a single man or woman in this here establishment that didn't lose someone because of you. Daniel Hayward…The Family's dog. How does it feel? Scurrying around with the rest of us."

He shakes the miners hand off from his shoulder with little effort. With a single glance, Daniel looks at the miner as if he were nothing.

"I wouldn't know."

The miner, shaken by the response takes his pint and begins to down the drink. Breathing deeper and more frantically through his nostrils, the ale begins to spill from the glass and runs down his chin. All the while the miner glares at Daniel, who pretends not to see him. Once

6

finished, the miner slams the glass onto the bar. His hand still tightly gripping it.

"Look around you," yelled the miner with a gargle in the back of his throat, "this place is hell! Dust covers our clothes, it's beneath out nails, gathers in our hair. It is in our lungs. Killing the weak, old and young. If they don't die because of the dust, then they'll die down in the mines. We brake our backs working so that we can have just enough to survive. None of us fought to keep this. We fought because if we didn't, even this ball of dirt would have been taken from us. Seven years and you have the nerve to look down on us. Your nothing but murdering scum."

The bar falls silent. Everyone watching the couple. Daniel notices the look on people's faces. Looks of anger, despair and a deep sadness. He can feel the tension in the bar. He closes his eyes and counts in his head.

One. Two. Three. Four…

This was supposed to be an easy job, Daniel thinks to himself.

Five. Six…

Daniel reclaims his composure. He limbers up by rolling his head from left to right. When he opens his eyes, he smiles at the miner. The grin across his face looks almost harmless.

"I just wanted to come in, take the weight off my feet and have a nice quiet drink. Here, let me buy you one of these. It's good stuff, from Earth no doubt," said Daniel, waving his whiskey about.

"Fuck you," screamed the miner.

Glass in hand, he throws his fist wildly towards Daniel's face. As if Daniel had rehearsed the scene before, both of his hands automatically raise to block the strike. The sound of glass shattering and a desperate scream of pain fills the bar.

Guarded by his coat, none of the pieces of glass penetrate the material, leaving him completely unharmed. He lowers his arms to finds the miner holding his hand, blood dripping on the floor.

Daniel approaches the emotional miner. Before he can offer help, he feels a stool brake against his back.

Stumbling forwards a few paces, Daniel turns and looks at the man behind him, gormlessly standing there with the broken stool legs. The man looks back and forth between Daniel and the legs, shocked that all that force had only set Daniel momentarily off balance. Once again, he raises what's left of the stool above his head, ready to take another swing.

Lightening quick, Daniel rushes in towards the man and plunges his fist under his ribs. Before he can even react, Daniel straightens up and throws another punch directly at his face. With the power behind the punch, the miner loses the strength in his legs and his face is lunched towards the bar. His head bounces off and a bloody print is left on the side.

At this point Daniel notices Freya's screams, but pays little care as he turns to the miner's friends who leap up from their seats to join the fight.

Each of them have a smirk across their face as they surround him. Slowly each of their nerves are shaken when they realise Daniel is smiling too. Breaking the standoff, one of the miners jolts forward only to be interrupted by the sound of a gunshot.

The men look at the end of the bar to find the owner holding a shotgun aimed at the ceiling. The barrel still smoking. As he lowers his aim, holding it steady waist high, the miners step back, returning to their seats.

"Everyone back down. Take a seat. The next round is on the house," he instructed to the pleasure of all the patrons. The owner then aims the gun towards Daniel. "You. Come with me."

Without arguing, Daniel walks towards the owner, ignoring the glaring eyes of the bar. The owner gestures to the door with an exit sign hung above it. Daniel opens it and glances back at the two he just had an encounter with. He nods gently to himself when he sees the miner picking himself up from the floor, blood still trickling down the side of his face.

"Freya, get the medical kit from behind the bar. I'll be back in a minute," instructed the owner further.

Stepping out into the backstreet, dust covers the pavement and once again he is met with the greyness of Jotunhiem. Behind him the owner waits in the doorway.

"What are you doing here?" asked the owner with a commanding tone.

"I'm here to see a guy called Loge. He has a job for me," he explained honestly.

"You'll find him in the underpasses of the town, if you've reached the smelting works, you've gone too far. You can find an entrance to the underpass just down there," said the owner while pointing to the end of the backstreet.

"I'm sure I can find it," Daniel thanked the owner as he begins walking off. After a few steps, Daniel turns back around and inspects his tattoo once more. "Why let me go?"

The owner mulls over his response for a few seconds.

9

"The war is over. I just want to be left alone and live out the rest of my days in peace."

"Peace?" questioned Daniel.

The owner chuckles as he returns to the bar.

*

Below the streets of the colony, the sound of heavy machinery and materials clanking against one another is deafening. The metallic roar echoes throughout the narrow underpass, an interconnecting maze that runs under the whole settlement. Daniel begins to question how any of the colonists manage to get a decent night's sleep with all this noise just underneath them.

The walls are cold blackened steel, the floor is covered with a thin carpeting layer of dust. Even in the underbelly of the colony, dust can be found. Dark, humid and it smells faintly of sewage.

Despite the conditions, it is far from being devoid of life. Venturing farther in he finds a small community of refugees living under the surface. Whole corridors and kicked in ventilation shafts have been sectioned off to establish living quarters. Old women slave over boiling pots of grey liquid. Sickly children run around playing chase, wheezing as they try to escape one another. Mothers stitch together old clothes. The lack of men hardly surprises Daniel.

Quarantined corridors house the bedridden. Coughing and spluttering colonists are tended to by the unqualified but caring. Dirty moist towels are used to dab the sick. The precious water is shared out sparingly. Those who have little time left are prayed for. A far too common sight.

10

Daniel makes his way through the community enquiring after Loge, every time receiving general directions to his apparent location.

Finally, Daniel turns a corner and is greeted with the scene of a man comforting a dying child. Loge stands out from the rest of the people with his fiery red beard and hair. He gently replaces the damp cloth over the boy's forehead, soothing the boy in a language Daniel does not know. He rinses the old cloth into a metal pan. A grey milky substance is squeezed out. The mother of the boy weeps.

Loge looks up to find Daniel watching him. As if snapping out of one role and into another, Loge grins and welcomes him.

"My friend, it has been a while. One year if I'm correct," Loge said while embracing Daniel.

Daniel barely moves, uncertain about the display of overfamiliarity.

"This is miserable," said Daniel into Loge's ear. "Who are these people?"

Loge steps back and holds him by his shoulders, not breaking eye contact with the ex-soldier.

"By now you must have seen this picture hundreds of times before? Refugees of the Purge. They must exist in the shadows, otherwise those accommodating them maybe subject to the same fate," explained Loge, surprised he had to explain their circumstance to the likes of Daniel.

"I've never seen it this bad before," elaborated Daniel, justifying his shock.

"Of course, you have. It's just been a long time since you cared to look. Things are bad for the Outer-Core and always have been. The Purge means whole settlements suddenly going dark. Then if some were lucky, in the following months survivors begin to arrive in neighbouring colonies. They bring with them mouths to feed, families to house and the sick to tend to. Each colony cannot simply declare they need more resources. Instead they are kept safe in places such as this. A cesspit of disease and hopelessness."

Loge guides Daniel through the underpass. Excitedly a group of children swarm the two men. First, they dance around Daniel, intrigued to find a new face and distract him whilst one of them rummages around in his coat pocket. Disappointed to only find a fistful of dust, the child is not discouraged and keeps on searching.

Daniel shoos them off. Amused at his discomfort, Loge draws their attention by reaching into his own pocket and pulls out half a loaf of stale bread. Thankful for the generosity, the children run off to share it.

They make their way through the busiest passes until they reach a room which was once used as maintenance storage. Loge holds the door open for him.

The lights flicker on, set off by motion sensors, and slowly the room is revealed. It is basic living quarters with beds and chairs fashioned from scrap material. Food and medical supplies are neatly stored on shelves.

"It is not much, but it is home for the time being," explained Loge, brushing passed to find out two clean-ish glasses. "Sorry I couldn't meet you at The Clacker, as you can imagine, something came up."

"Don't worry about it," Daniel dismissed.

Loge pours two generous measures from an unlabelled bottle. He hands Daniel the drink.

Wary of the contents of the glass, he sniffs the liquid before sipping it. The same smoky whiskey hits his senses that he'd just brought in the bar. Daniel figures the bottle at the bar must have been a gift from Loge for the community putting him up.

"They are rough boys, but good at heart," said Loge, somehow knowing what had transpired earlier. He falls into an armchair, stretching his feet out to the metal tub acting as a coffee table. "But you're not here for any of this. Let me tell you about the job. Take a seat."

Loge offers out his hand, directing Daniel to the chair besides him. Perching himself on the edge, Daniel is surprised at how comfortable the chair is. Regardless of comfort however, he refuses to sit back any farther. He attempts to brush himself down, only to realise the futility in doing so.

"West from here, hidden within a crater, is a miner's colony known to the locals as The Golden Ring. A name forgotten by the rest of the Charted Systems. It is technically the oldest functioning mining facility in the Charted Systems and it was once the most profitable. A few months ago, the Golden Ring fell silent. All communication fell dead and not a single merchant has returned. The people here were waiting for the inevitable trickle of refugees. But no one came. Other nearby colonists were planning on taking the colony for themselves. Anyone who controls the Golden Ring would be the most powerful force on Jotunhiem. There have been several excursions to scout and secure the settlement. Again no one came back. At first, people thought it could have been Loyalist soldiers killing on sight," began Loge.

"But, you have no interest in the colony," interrupted Daniel.

Having been occupied by swirling the liquid around the glass, Daniel is startled to look up and see Loge leaning in, only inches away from his own face.

From a distance, Loge could be described as hansom man with defined features that can only come from age. Up close however, his bone structure seems acutely sharp. His skin appears to be stretched across his face, giving the appearance that Loge is wearing someone else's skin. Daniel puts it down to the planet's atmosphere being very dry and unforgiving.

"You are cleverer than you look. That's why I like you Daniel. Keep them guessing, personas are deadlier than a bullet from a gun," said Loge excitedly.

Daniel finally sits back and slowly brings the drink to his lips.

"I'm not sure about that," he quipped back at the comment.

"Well, anyhow, your right. I'm not interested in causing pointless bloodshed for these people," said Loge. "Have you heard the rumours of a dreadnought so large it could not fit through the EMRs? A ship so large that if it were to enter the gravitational pull of a planet, it would begin to bend due to its sheer size. A dreadnought that has defied the Brasil Agreement and has a deadlier arsenal than the Sisters combined."

"I've heard a lot of rumours in my time. People talked about a ghost who would slaughter the weak of the battlefield. That a single bird was responsible for the outbreak of the Revolt on Maia. I often find the truth behind most these stories to be far more subdue and less fantastical then they first appear," said Daniel with a degree of smugness. "I've never heard of this great serpent that lingers in the deepest depths of the Chartered

System. What has it got to do with Jotunhiem and the Golden Ring?"

"There was, a particular individual who lived in the colony. He spent the last quarter of a century hiding from the PeaceSeekers. He was once an engineer for the Mad Son, employed to design a dreadnought to face off against the Mother. His designs are valuable," admitted Loge. "In the wrong hands, those designs could be catastrophic. However, if they could find themselves in the hands of a friend…"

"So, you want me to go and obtain the schematics to this supposed ship? Sounds a little uneventful. Not to mention absolutely pointless. No one here willing to cash in an extra pay check?" enquired Daniel perplexed.

"That's because it is only half the job," said Loge, then he takes a sip of his whiskey. "You'll need to take the designs to Neo-Shanxi. An acquaintance of mine going by the name 'Mr Han' owns a dress making shop in the Political District. He is already waiting for you."

Daniel finishes his drink and places the glass down on the metal tub. Feeling angry and slightly deceived he contemplates whether it is worth the risk. Daniel has not been to Neo-Shanxi in five years and for good reason.

"Do you have our payment?" he asked emotionlessly.

"Your payment can be received upon delivery," Loge replied.

Daniel stands up from his seat and grabs the bottle of whiskey from the table.

"West?"

"West. If you follow the underpass left from here, it'll take you to an abandoned underground railway. It originally began construction when Jotunhiem was under the control of the Three Sons, but because of the war it never saw completion. The railway should take you most the way. Once it ends, continue straight from there. Eventually you'll see the crater, don't attempt to transverse it. If you've gone straight enough you'll come across a tunnel that will take you through to the Golden Ring."

"How do I find his place when I get there? What exactly am I looking for?" asked Daniel.

Loge looks at him with a mischievous grin.

"Something tells me that won't be a problem when you get there. Trust your instincts. It's half the reason I hired you."

Loge lifts himself from his chair to find out a bag and fills it with a couple of flasks of water and the other half of the stale loaf of bread. The bag is zipped closed, then held out for Daniel to take.

Daniel does not say anything in response. Instead looks at Loge with a level of contentment before snatching the bag and abruptly heading for the door.

Left from the maintenance storage room, the underpass continues straight for what seems like miles. Further away from the congregated community, the underpass becomes darker and damper. The smell of sewage is replaced with a metallic cleanness. Eventually Daniel is wandering around in complete blackness. He holds his arm out, letting the palm of his hand brush along the wall, guiding each of his steps. Drips of water echo in the darkness.

Suddenly, a light begins to flicker at the end of the pass. Seeming some distance away, Daniel is surprised at how quick he arrives at the source. The light illuminates a big heavy metal door. There is no indication that the door is in anyway locked. Preparing himself for a struggle, he grips the handle and tugs at it.

Opening with ease, Daniel stumbles backwards as the steel door swings towards him.

On the other side is a huge tunnel dimly lit by red florescent safety lights running along either side. The blackened steel of the underpass continues, absorbing the light, making it look darker than it is. Several electromagnetic rail lines run through the tunnel.

The sheer scale of the construction indicates the ambitions for the colony. So far everything looks fully built and operational, Daniel wonders to himself why the rail system was never used. It was not like the Three Sons to ever scrimp on their plans.

Stepping down from the underpass to the tracks, Daniel checks both directions. Each way is swallowed in darkness. Neither way gives any indication of ever reaching an end. Uncertain which way is west, Daniel stands still in contemplation, attempting to mentally retraces his steps to come to an educated guess which direction he should head.

A faint breeze tickles Daniel's left hand. Without question, he begins to walk alongside the rails.

For hours Daniel wanders through the underground railway with no end in sight. For the best part of his waking day he's been walking. He is starting to feel the strain. Every now and then he stops to take a swig of the whiskey. Progressively the taste becomes sickening. Tiredness hangs over him. A numb pain slowing his pace.

Red lights. Black steel. Straight tracks. Every mile looks the same. A feeling of being lost in a continuous loop plagues Daniel's thoughts.

With no end in sight for today, Daniel finds a dark spot to get some rest in. With his back against the wall, his head becomes heavier and his eyes slowly begin to close.

*

Gunshots can be heard in the far distance. Imminently Daniel sits upright and searches his surroundings. The heaviness of his head makes him feel off balance. He realises it's because of his helmet. Dressed head to toe in body armour, the weight takes a moment for him to adjust. Looking down he notices he'd fallen asleep with rifle in hand.

The air is cold and smells of concrete and gunpowder. Around Daniel are other Loyalist soldiers. Alarmed, they jump to their feet and get into position. The building they are in is half blown away. Scorch marks mark the cement and tiles. Bullet holes riddle the remaining structure. A hand is placed on his left shoulder, startling Daniel.

"*Calm down soldier*," said a deep mechanically muffled voice in Chinese.

Kneeling next to him is their commander, Knox Jung. A hulk of a man and monstrously so.

Unlike the rest of the units in the squad, Knox is dressed in black and steel grey body armour, well fitted and unique. The black skin-tight exoskeleton suit seems to pulsate, as if the suit itself were alive. Thick, heavy looking, grey body armour covers vital areas. Though they are bulking slabs of protection, his movement is completely unhindered. Hanging from Knox's waist is what can only be described as a skirt, two lose pieces of black leather covering half of each leg. The bottom of his face is covered by a mask that is integrated with the rest of the suit. Wires and tubes run from his back, around his neck and connects to the mask. Covering the rest of his head is a face mask with large red lenses.

"It has not yet begun. The gun fire is from a few blocks away, they have reached the blockade. Come we must make our move," Knox informed Daniel.

Daniel simply nods in full understanding of what is being asked of him. Cautiously he brings himself to his feet, keeping his height level to the wall he was sleeping against.

There is pause as they wait for further instructions.

Without a word, their commander points two figures towards the staircase signalling to 'move out'. Knox leads with a pace that is initially hard to keep up with. The squad organises itself and follows close behind. Daniel takes his position second to their commander. Each of the men and women are battle-hardened, hand-picked and, above all, loyal.

They move down the stairs to street level, making as little noise as possible. The buildings around them become alive with shadows moving in the night. Other Loyalist squads take their positions. Exiting the building into the open, Knox raises his fist. Daniel and the rest of the squad imminently stop.

Almost as if he could sense the advancement of the enemy in the disruption of the air, Knox gives the signal to take cover. Scattering, each of the soldiers find safety behind rubble or climb over into abandoned homes and shops.

Daniel rests against a collapsed building on the opposite side of the street to is his commander. For a second, Daniel swears he makes eye contact from behind those

19

red lenses. It is quickly dismissed as Knox nods forward, reminding Daniel to focus.

On the ground besides him, he notices a body lying dead in a dried pool of blood. Though the body is mangled, it wears civilian clothes. He must have been a causality of the conflict this morning.

Suddenly, Daniel is taken by a sense of unease, unsure whether his eyes are playing tricks on him.

The dead body reanimates. From the corpse, loud groans and spluttering begins to resonate in the silence of the street. Shocked, Daniel looks around to his fellow soldiers for advice.

Before he can get an answer, a hand weakly grasps his leg. Gawking at Daniel, the not so dead corpse smiles and beings to laugh a gargled laugh. In his other hand, the civilian presents an unpinned grenade.

Just as it is about to explode, an unhuman force carries Daniel away to safety.

*

Daniel awakes in a panic, frantically waving his arms about. It takes a good few seconds for him to distinguish reality from dream. Gasping for breath, the first sobering sensation is his dry mouth. He finds out a flask of water from the bag and begins to gulp it all down.

Half empty, he stops himself and remembers that he must drink it sparingly. Feeling as exhausted as he was when he fell asleep, Daniel concludes that perhaps he had only slept for a couple of hours. However, the tunnel no longer seems so dark. Farther down, daylight creeps in. Daniel had walked until the early hours of the morning. Dust has gathered in the crevices of his coat and for the first time on this planet Daniel is thankful to see the grey dirt.

The groans from his stomach remind him that he should eat. Daniel takes no pleasure in eating the stale bread, but understands he will need the energy to cross the dust to reach the Golden Ring.

After an unsatisfying breakfast, he strips down to his underwear and shakes out the dust from his clothes. Clouds of grey are carried off down the tunnel.

His body is a canvas of scars and burns. A story once went with each one, but as time passes they have lost meaning. Muscle has been forged through circumstance, his stature lean but intimidating. No one usually intends on picking a fight with him. Before redressing he climbs over the other side of the tracks to relieve himself.

Buttoning up the last button on his shirt, Daniel then picks up his coat. Inspecting the initials 'C.J.' stitched in the inside collar, a sadness weighs down heavy on him. Throwing it on, he picks up the bag and continues towards the light at the end of the tunnel.

At the end of the tunnel, he notices the familiar twisted metal and destruction of war. Daniel had been confused why the railways were inoperable, now it is painfully obvious. Dust blankets the opening of the tunnel. Daniel stands looking out at a clam desert of dust, on the horizon is the crater.

From his pocket a quiet melody begins to play. Daniel reaches for a wireless ear piece and answers the call.

"Pilot, is everything OK?" asked Daniel concerned.

"Everything is fine here, what happened to you? You went off the sensors for the whole night. We were worried about you," said Pilot equally concerned. Her pronunciation of every word is perfect, her tone warm and yet assured.

"Yeah, I was walking in some abandoned underground rail system all night," explained Daniel.

"We could of came and picked you up," said Pilot as if it were self-evident.

"Not possible. I'm heading into a dark zone. We shouldn't give our presence away. Stay where you are, I'll be back by this evening," ordered Daniel.

"Understood Captain. We are here on standby if you need us," Pilot reassured him, then hangs up.

Daniel removes the ear piece and places it back into his coat pocket. Taking in the desolate view, he sighs.

A cool, slow, refreshing breeze sweeps through his hair. Only a small amount of dust is unsettled. With the sun baring down, Daniel decides not to do up his coat and begins his descent down to the dust that stands between him and the Golden Ring.

*

Arriving at the foot of the crater, the tunnel's opening looks nothing more than a black dot in a sea of grey. Just as Loge said, he did the best he could to travel in a straight line. Quickly Daniel realises what it is that he should be searching for. He beings to climb, but only as far as where he imagines the level of the railway to be.

Every step he takes, his feet sink into the dust. Falling on his hands, Daniel continues to scale the foot of the crater on all fours.

After a few yards, his hands are dry and sore. The dirt begins to push up into his finger nails. Daniel checks to see whether his fingers are bleeding, he is relieved to see that they are not. He leaps to reach new heights, the ground is disturbed, irritating his eyes. Daniel presses on undeterred.

He feels the surface under him change density. Sweeping away the dust, a blackened steel hatch is reviled. Unsure if he was fatigued from the climb, the digging, or whether the hatch is as stiff as it feels, Daniel struggles to lift the hunk of metal open. The hinges screech a metallic cry.

Precariously he searches for his footing on the ladder. With every step down, the same neon red darkness engulfs him. Following his descent into darkness is a trickle of dust that runs over his head.

At the other end of the tunnel is another opening. No door, no station. Just an opening overlooking the crater.

Daniel approaches the edge and is met with a refreshing view of a clear sky, rocky earth and an almost illusionary golden shimmer that glistens in the morning sun. The geological scar is ancient, the meteor having hit Jotunhiem hundreds of years before humans colonised the planet.

Thanks to the clear air, Daniel feels as if he has clarity of thought and for the first time since he has woken up he feels sober. Sitting in the middle of the impact is the mining colony. Though a sizable settlement, it pales into insignificance compared to its surroundings.

Clambering down from the protruding rail system, Daniel lands hard on the rocks below. His fall is cumbersome. With no one around, he saves himself any embarrassment.

Shaking it off, he begins to map his way down to the centre. The rocks are loose and every so often Daniel disrupts the unstable earth, which slides out from under him. Much of his decent is comprises of skating uncontrollably, only just maintaining his balance.

The crater's rim is tall enough to hold back the winds that drag the dust across the land. The difference is uncanny. The whole landscape seems to feel unnatural and out of place. It is something that never cases to perplex Daniel, the diversity of each world he has visited. But to seek the reason why, does not interest him. Even if it did, he is convinced that he would not be able to understand it.

No cloud of dust means that the atmosphere cannot retain its heat. Daniel's breath becomes viable. Despite the sudden chill, he perseveres without doing up his coat, welcoming the cooler temperature.

Walking in the middle of the street, a sense of unease washes over him. The colony is totally lifeless. The lack of wind means everything hangs static. There is no humming of machinery; no hustle of trade; no boisterous cheers from the local; no lights on in people's homes. The colony has no pulse.

The cerement buildings look identical to the other colony, only cleaner. The uniform layout is comforting to Daniel. Already he has assumptions of where things are. It is the same as any mining colony in the Outer Core, pre-planned and systematic.

Building after building, nothing. Daniel attempts another home. He grabs the handle of the front door, already knowing it's not locked. There are no signs of forced entry, distress or resistance. Everything has just been left there.

The people who lived here clearly took pride in themselves. Next to the sink all the dishes are stacked neatly. Their sofas facing towards one another rather than

24

at the television screen. Each tablet in its charging dock ready for the next user. Daniel picks up an electronic frame, it has little charge left, but he can just about make out the family photos flickering on the screen. Mother, father, daughter and son.

Daniel's ears twitch as small footsteps patter about at the front door. Turning to face them, he is surprised to find no one there.

Throwing the frame onto sofa, he runs outs of the house and searches the street. Daniel stops to find a small girl scurrying off around the corner. Without question, he follows.

In the centre of town, he comes across three children in the middle of the empty street. Two of the children are playing a game which no longer seems to excite them and the third is trying to warn them about the stranger. Despite his efforts to approach them quietly, they notice him straight away.

"Hey mister! Do you want to play with us?" the eldest one asked.

Daniel is unsure if the child is male or female. The boyish features could belong to either sex.

"Hey! He's the one I was just telling you about," said the girl.

Clearly the middle child, her hair blonde and she wears a beautiful pink and green dress. A style of dress no longer worn, belonging in books regarding Germanic history.

Ignoring the protest of the girl, Daniel joins the children. Each of them are scarred, as if whole veins have been cut out from under the skin. Red vine like scars ascend from their body, up their necks and fade as they reach their face. It's a sight all too familiar in the Charted Systems.

"What game are we playing?" Daniel asked the eldest child.

"Marbles. I found them in my Dad's old chest. He said it was passed down to him from his Grandfather who was from Earth. Can you believe! I'm related to someone from Earth," he said with a revitalised enthusiasm.

Daniel smiles at the child amused.

"My Mum said that Earth deserves to have gone dark because they abandoned us here," the small one stated.

The third child is small and fragile, unkempt and underfed. Though the child must be no more than seven, he does not act so. In fact, none of the children act as children.

"I think you have to get the small ones closest to the big one," explained the middle child.

"You know mister, a lot of people have come here since it happened," said the eldest child.

"Since what happened?" Daniel fainted ignorance.

"Since..." the middle child began. Her eyes begin to swell with tears, both the other children notice her reaction, but are somewhat apathetic to it.

"Shhh..." interrupted the youngest child, trying to continue their game.

Daniel decides not to pursue the issues, he already knows none of the children would have any knowledge of what happened to them. Instead he watches patiently as they continue to play their game of marbles.

The colony is still. Silent. Despite this Daniel feels as if they are being watched. Before he can ask anything, the youngest child looks up from their game and gives Daniel an unsettling look.

"Why are you here?"

"Don't be so rude," snapped the eldest.

"But why are you here?" continued the middle child.

"Everyone who comes here dies," explained the youngest.

"It all started when we woke up," the middle child muttered despondently.

"Shut up, he's here to play with us. Don't make him leave," said the eldest irritably.

Daniel attempts the defuse the situation by taking a marble and rolls it towards the largest marble, knocking several other marbles out the way however gets nowhere near the large one.

Accepting himself as a novice at the game, he looks up at the children.

"I'm just passing by," he lied.

"Why are you here?" the youngest asked again, ignoring Daniel's messily attempt to deceive them.

"Why are you here?" repeated the middle child.

"Are you here to play with us?" asked the eldest hopefully.

The youngest interrupted, not giving Daniel a chance to speak, "It's dangerous for adults to stay here."

"Some nice people tried to take us with them," continued the middle child.

"But they died too," said the eldest.

"He will kill anyone who tries to take the Golden Ring," finished the youngest.

"Who will?" Daniel asked unexpectedly captivated.

"He is albino," said the middle child.

"He is the reason why we have food," said the youngest.

"He looks after us," admitted the eldest.

Before they could continue Daniel interjected with a half honest question, "My friend knew someone who used to live here. Said he was an amazing inventor. Don't suppose you knew anyone like that?"

The children look at one another.

"You should go," said the middle child. She opens her clenched fist and drops the marbles she was concealing. Rising to her feet, she turns her back and begins to walk off.

The eldest looks back and forth between Daniel had their friend. Eventually she nudges Daniel.

"*Psst*...I know where you can find his home. He was a strange man. Most the other children in the town never liked going around there. I can take you."

"He will die," warned the youngest.

"Mister, will you die?"

"I haven't yet," explained Daniel with a good-humoured confidence.

"Good, don't die today."

They leave the youngest vacantly starring at the marbles.

Skipping through the streets, the eldest child seems to have reverted, acting too young for her age. Following her, Daniel cannot seem to match her pace, every step he takes seems to be out of sync. Occasionally he falls behind, sometimes he races ahead.

Coming to an abrupt holt, she points to the house across the street. Instinctively Daniel knows it's the place. A three-storey building standing out from all the rest. Turning to thank the child, she has already gone.

Inside, nothing has been disturbed since the Purge, just as with the family home. The ground floor is basic. A single armchair. A kitchen with basic facilities. What is striking are the real paper books on the shelves. Something Daniel has seen before, but an unusual sight on such a colony.

Walking over to the kitchen, he tests the taps. Not much more than a dribble of water comes out. Daniel then places his bag down on the coffee table and begins searching for the blueprints.

Heading upstairs to the second floor, there is shift in the weight of the air. Daniel becomes cautious of his surroundings. The whole floor is one room. Boards are littered with diagrams and designs, while desks have calculations spalled across them.

A frame on one of the shelves catches his attention. It contains an actual photograph. Interested in such a rare find, Daniel, on closer inspection, realises who is in the picture. On the right is a man, early fifties, rough and Scandinavian looking. He assumes this to be the man whose home he is currently in. Embraced in his arms is a man with fiery red hair, it could not be mistaken as anybody other than Loge, but much younger, before Daniel ever knew him.

Concluding that this job is not as simple as he had first anticipated, he is disrupted by the cold click of the hammer of a gun being pulled back.

Unthreatened, he turns to face the gun. A solemn smirk stretches across his face as he discovers a child on the other end. No more than a teenager, the Chinese boy's skin and hair is washed of colour. The kid wears a black raincoat with highlights of red and gold. On his left arm is a band with the PeaceSeeker emblem. A red and gold circle with two smaller ones orbiting it, one in the top left, the other in the bottom right, in the centre is the Chinese character for '*peace*'. The fact that the boy has not already pulled the trigger let's Daniel know he will be walking away alive.

"You are Daniel Hayward?" the PeaceSeeker asked nervously in Chinese.

Silence as they stand there, neither one willing to move. The boy tries to work out Daniel's smirk.

"Fuck...I cannot believe they allow kids to become PeaceSeekers now. What has Bình let it become?" Daniel mocked.

Another moment of silence follows while Daniel waits for a response.

"Do not tell me. She promised you that if you could kill me, she would make you into some great hero of the Loyalists. Or better yet, you came from some backwater colony that just so happened to be chosen to be Purged, and she gave you an out. In exchange for my death, you get go to Maia and undergo training to become one of them?" Daniel rambled on.

The PeaceSeeker re-steadies his aim. *"They said you talk."*

"You do not?" retorted Daniel.

"You are Daniel Hayward," restated the albino child.

Before the kid can even react, Daniel grabs the barrel of the gun, repositioning it directly at his own forehead. Having closed the gap, there is now very little distance between them. Calmly and vigilantly he watches the boy for any slight twitch.

"Would it even matter if I was not Daniel Hayward?" he asked.

"No."

The gunshot is deafening.

Not used to the sound of gunfire in an enclosed space, the albino child squints as the ringing in his ears causes him immense discomfort. Eyes closed, he tries to pull back the pistol. But the more he tugs, the more resistance he encounters.

Daniel holds the gun high above his own head, totally unscathed by the bullet. The kid tries his best to wrestle it out of his grasp, unable match Daniel's strength. Keeping Daniel preoccupied, the albino throws out a kick, using all his weight to try and separate the two of them.

Stumbling backwards, the child is about to fire off another round. But before he can take aim, Daniel has already run up to the PeaceSeeker and lays his fist into the kid's chest.

Winded, the kid is too stunned to fight back and Daniel takes his arm, twisting it in an unnatural manner. Something in his arm pops and the gun falls to the floor with a thud.

The PeaceSeeker reaches with his free hand for a small hidden blade in his boot. Swinging into the pain, the albino plunges the knife between Daniel's ribs.

Manically the child sneers as he forces the knife upwards, but Daniel feels nothing. Confused the boy sees that his blade has not penetrated the coat's material. Daniel smiles cheekily, then strikes the albino with the back of his hand.

His feet try to carry him away, but he only gets so far before realising his other arm is still in Daniel's vice like grip. Unable to escape any farther, he thinks to kick his way out. Before he can even fully extend his leg out, he is pulled in towards Daniel. His only leg on the ground is swept away and his face connects with Daniel's fist. The albino slams to the floor.

"*Stay down,*" Daniel warned the child, still twisting his wrist.

The pistol is right beside him and the PeaceSeeker grabs the gun, firing wildly at Daniel. It is kicked out of his hand before he can unload a few lucky shots.

Daniel stomps his heel in the kid's face to stop him from squirming about. Blood seeps from the albino's gums. Placing a knee into his rib cage, Daniel leans in close.

"Let me get what I need and let me leave. I do not want to have to kill you."

The PeaceSeeker pokes Daniel in the eyes with his free hand and the weight pinning him down shifts as Daniel, equally hurt as he is shocked, regroups from the attack. Daniel checks his sight. Though blurry, it will recover.

Working on sound rather than his vision, he traces the child's movement as they both climb to their feet. With his hands shielding his eyes, Daniel delivers a powerful kick. The force sends the albino flying down the stairs. The boy tumbles down one step at a time.

Not allowing the PeaceSeeker to gain the advantage by finding somewhere to hide, Daniel makes his way to the ground floor. He can just about make out the child at the bottom step, already recovering from the fall.

Before the child can get back up, Daniel's foot lands squarely in the boy's chest.

"Stay down."

In defiance, the PeaceSeeker attempts to get back up. Again, Daniel kicks the boy. The blow hits the child directly in his face. Blood splatters across the room. The albino's lip is split and his nose broken. Red dribbles out from his mouth.

"Stay down."

Feeling convinced that he has put an end to the child's fight, Daniel turns back to the stairs. But as soon as he turns his back, he can hear the albino charging at him.

Spinning to meet the child with his fists, he is instead tackled against the fridge. The boy begins to swing madly at Daniel. Unfazed by each hit, Daniel simply overpowers the child and places him in a headlock.

"*Stand down,*" insisted Daniel.

The albino ignores him.

"*Stand down.*"

The PeaceSeeker sinks his finger nails into Daniel's face. Feeling the burn as his skin brakes, Daniel tightens his hold around the boy's neck.

"*Stand down,*" pleaded Daniel to the child one last time.

His finger nails find Daniel's eyes. Enduring the pain for long enough, he recognises that the PeaceSeeker won't give up. In one sharp jerk, Daniel snaps the albino boy's neck. The body in his grasp goes limp. The hand clawing his face falls away slowly. Only when Daniel is sure does he let go.

Leaving the boy's body resting up against the refrigerator, he heads over to his bag and finds out the bottle of whiskey. Taking a seat in the armchair, Daniel opens the unlabelled bottle and takes a huge swig.

While he catches his breath, he watches the dead body on the other side of the room. Unable to think of any fitting words to say to alleviate the contradicting clash of emotions, he just sits there and takes another drink.

Blood trickles down his face. Slamming the bottle down, Daniel heads over to the kitchen sink to clean his wounds. Only drops of water come from the tap, though it is enough to dampen a cloth with.

Dabbing the scratches, he winces at the sharp sting. He catches his reflection in the window and is surprised at how deep the child had sunk his nails in. Doing his best with the little he has, Daniel knows he will have to seek more attention soon so it doesn't become infected. As he wrings the cloth, red and grey droplets stain the sink.

Upstairs again, he resumes his search for the blueprints, this time he has a good idea of where to find them. He picks up the photo of the stranger and a young Loge. After one last look at the photograph itself, he turns the frame around and opens it. Sure enough, tapped to the back is a memory card. Next to the card is a message:

Our last hope that will end the reign of the one-eyed bitch, Jörmungandr.

Daniel stands there confused, unsure of Loge's alliance or motives. Unsure of the purpose of him being here. Concerned about the complications of his job. Instead of tearing off the memory card, he takes the photograph as well, placing it neatly into his pocket. Daniel decides he will need to confront Loge about the nature of these blueprints.

The colony is silent. Static. As if time has stopped and the colonists vanished. The sun high in the sky. Despite this, without the blanket of dust trapping the heat, it is bitterly cold. The crater sparkles. It is as if he were in the centre of a golden ring.

Left in the middle of the street are a set of marbles. No one there to play with them. Static. Frozen in time. Waiting for the next move to be made.

*

Daniel kicks open the door to the maintenance storage room. But no one is there. Nothing is there. All Loge's comforts, supplies and resources are gone. Daniel stares at an empty room. All that remains are the upturned metal tub and an unopened bottle of whiskey. Taking the bottle, Daniel exits the room and wanders up to the surface.

Walking into The Clacker, he is met with angry and fearful faces. One of the miners in the bar has his hand wrapped in bandages.

Sitting alone at the bar is the old man who he first spoke to upon arriving at the colony. Ignoring the tension in the room, Daniel takes a seat next to him. Freya smiles uneasily at Daniel. He orders a shot of the expensive whiskey.

"Don't suppose you could extended a favour to an old man, could you?" asked the miner.

"Sure, don't see the harm," Daniel replied. He looks behind and catches the glares from the group he had a run in with. "Hey, could I just buy the bottle? And can I get six glasses with that?"

"There you are honey," said Freya as she places the bottle and six glasses out in front of him.

Daniel pours himself and the old man a generous measure, then carries the rest over to the table of miners. He lays out the glasses and places down the bottle.

"No hard feelings about the other night," said Daniel.

They grumble under their breath, but accept the token of apology nevertheless.

At the bar, the old man swirls the liquid around until the whole glass has a thin coat of whiskey. Taking his time, he places it under his nose and gently inhales. The warmth of the aroma makes the old man groan in satisfaction.

"Heard you caused trouble," the old man japed.

"Well you know what they say about men who come in from the dust," Daniel said back in the same manner. "It seems like there is enough trouble without my being here. Jotunhiem is going through hard times."

"Aren't we all?"

"I guess."

"We do the best we can for people. Hope that if it happens to us, people would do their best in return. In times like these, it's important to retain our humanity. Isn't that all we can ask for?"

"I assume Loge skipped town?" Daniel asked, ignoring the old man's comment.

"You mean the red-haired fellow? Yeah, he comes and goes. Never too sure when to expect him next," said the old man.

"I'd expect you'll be seeing him sooner rather than later this time," he explained.

With one large gulp Daniel finishes his drink. From his wallet, he pulls out the emerald card and places it besides the old man on the bar. "Here."

"What is this?"

"Think of it as a back-door key to The Family's treasury. If you're careful enough, you'll never get caught. I haven't yet."

The old man stares at him shocked. "How could you just give something like this away?"

"I'm not giving it away," said Daniel. "I'll be back for it. Besides, favours tend to be worth more than money these days, so don't consider this as a free loan. Just make sure those people down there are well fed."

"Who would even accept these credits?" questioned the old man.

"Smugglers, black markets. The only ones you can trust to be honest when it comes to money. There are a few large neighbouring settlements that'll have what you need. They're not hard to find either. I expect most the younger people around here trade a few things here and there when they make shipments. They'll know," explained Daniel.

He jumps off his stool and just as he is about to leave, taps his fist on the bar, remembering there is one last thing he must do.

"By the way. There were three children who survived the Purge of the Golden Ring. Water is running low and I doubt they can hold out for much longer," Daniel informed the old man.

"Consider it done," the old man smiled.

And with that Daniel walks out of the bar, though the grey streets of the colony and back into the dust in which he came.

*

Almost buried by the dust sits the Mazu, a small craft which Daniel has learnt to call home. Four wings protrude from its body, the span unnecessarily long for the boat and the front wings inverted. What seems like two blades extend far out beyond the nose. The cockpit's shutters are down protecting the glass from being scratched. None of the edges are smooth or perfectly curved, almost everything about the boat seems to defy aerodynamics and yet in the hands of Pilot it manoeuvres unlike any other dual craft. On Jotunhiem the black of the Mazu contrasts with the dust, but in the depth of space it disappears completely.

Climbing the docking door at the back, Daniel is met by Yuri in the airlock. The young man is blessed with unusually rugged hansom Slavic features. His hair shaved, his cheeks still youthfully smooth. Yuri holds out a clear bag with an air seal along the top.

"Pilot said you have to strip down and place your clothes in the bag," Yuri relayed the message.

Daniel laughs and begins to take off his coat. "Nice to see you too."

"Don't complain, unless you want to clean out clogged up machinery...Captain," said Pilot over the intercom.

"I promise I won't look," joked Yuri.

Dressing down to his underwear Daniel places each item of clothing in the bag. Once it is sealed, the airlock opens and the two step inside the Mazu.

Running down the centre is a tight dark, metallic corridor leading to a living space at the front of the craft. The interior is clean and well-kept despite the boat showing its age. History has stained the surfaces with deep dark red splashes. Patterns can be identified, depicting abstract stories of events that long preceded Daniel and his crew. The limited lighting coming from the floor and ceiling is enough for people to navigate where they are going, but offers little else. On each side of the corridor are three compartments. The doors look heavy, but slide open effortlessly.

Yuri turns to the first compartment on his right. "I will give these to Ben to clean up for you."

Thanking him with a nod, Daniel continues to the next compartment on the right. Entering his quarters, he throws off his underwear and turns on the shower. Knowing that water is a limited commodity since the purifier busted, he steps in before it's had a chance to warm up. Scrubbing hard, he gets the dust out from every crevice.

A game of Chaupar between Ben and Pilot is put on hold as their captain joins them in the living quarters.

With only three years' difference between her and Daniel, Pilot's experience of the war was similar as they both served in the last few years of the conflict. South Asian, Pilot always wears her long dark hair up and is more comfortable in her old pilot's uniform than in civvies.

Ben on the other hand has started to go grey. Wrinkles define his mahogany face. From his neck down, scars cover his body. Scars not to dissimilar from the young children in the Golden Ring.

Taking a seat at the table, Daniel waits for Yuri to finish brewing the tea.

"You look tired," said Ben.

"Nothing that a good cup of tea won't fix," Yuri called out from across the room.

"Did you make contact with Loge?" asked Pilot.

"Yeah."

"And?"

"Did we get paid?" asked Yuri as he brings over the pot of tea. He pours everyone a cup before taking a seat.

"Not yet."

"Oh," remarked Pilot.

"Are we getting paid?" joked Ben.

"The job is not quite done yet. Loge said we can pick up our payment at the same time we deliver the goods," explained Daniel. Tasting his tea, he smiles. "That is damn fine."

"It is only the dried-out leaves from the last pot...and the pot before that," said Yuri confused.

"He's pulling your leg kid," said Ben. He takes a sip of his own and shudders at the foul tasteless liquid.

The four of them sit in silence as they drink. The bright and vibrant colours of the living quarters make the boat seem more homily. Blankets and silks that they have acquired over the years cover the seats and are pinned to the hull. Each decorated with a different Chinese, Indian or Arabic patterns.

"Where are we headed off to then?" asked Pilot.

"Neo-Shanxi."

His crew are shocked. Yuri chokes on his tea, thumping his fist against his chest. Each of them turn to look at one another, hoping that someone else will challenge their captain.

"We are not that desperate. The old girl has more in her than we're giving her credit. Let's hold off the repairs. There is bound to be someone in the Charted Systems that can have a look at her," protested Ben.

Daniel glances over at Pilot. "You know as well as I do that we don't have many options left. If we turn this down we run the risk of getting left a drift."

As dangerous as Neo-Shanxi is, she knows the captain is right. The Mazu is not your run of the mill spacecraft. Few people know of its existence, even fewer could ever hope to understand it's design. Parts, along with able mechanics, are rare. Placing her cup on the table, she tightens the straps around her gloves.

"Buckle up," she sighed.

Pilot leaves the table and climbs the ladder to the cockpit. Yuri rushes to pack away the teapot and cups. He pours away the dregs of the tea and is a little dismayed to be throwing away the leaves too. Ben gathers up the pieces of the game and puts them neatly away in the draw underneath the table, making a mental note of Pilot's strategy.

With everything securely locked away, Ben and Yuri re-join Daniel and strap themselves in. Over the intercom, Pilot confirms everyone is ready.

Once satisfied she flips the switch and the Mazu begins to hum. The boat shakes as it lifts off the ground.

One last time Pilot confirms their destination.

"Captain?"

"Neo-Shanxi."

THE FAMILY

OPERATION BA'AL

Earth

Magpie

The rain has left an acidic taste in the back of her throat. Though the night is bitter, it has been a long time since she has felt the cold. Above New York City, the sky is stained with a pale pea green tinge. The lights of the city twinkle. Up on the rooftops, there is a calming silence.

A scar forms a crater in her cheek, it is one of countless many wounds that she has collected in her long years of service. Her hood flaps in the wind. Through the scope of her rife she watches the silhouetted figure in the hotel room across the road.

"Do you see him?" asked Wolf in her ear.

Magpie lets the trigger go and presses the communication piece closer to her ear.

"Affirmative, awaiting further orders," she replied, her French accent makes such a cold response seem somehow poetic.

Under the rain mac she hides her identity. On her chest, an emblem with the letters S.E.L. Few people have ever heard of the division. Even fewer know it's purpose.

"What is he doing?" asked Wolf.

Magpie watches the man through the scope carefully. Mesmerised, she follows the figure as he paces up and down the room.

In the wind, she is sure she can hear strings of an ancient musical instrument being plucked. Each note played sounds as it were fighting against a typhoon just to be heard. She beings to fill lightheaded. Her finger returns to the trigger.

Thoughts rush through her mind, it would take nothing more than a second of defiance and she could end it all here and now. Visions blind her slight. Images so lucid they seem more than mere imagination or dream. Red and gold liquids unveil a past yet unlived.

A man stands naked surrounded by flames. Crawling along his skin is a dragon. The breath of fire from the creature scorches the man's face, obscuring his beauty. As he burns away, all that remains are three stars slowly colliding with one another, tearing each other apart from the strength of their gravitational pull. The destruction of the stars stokes the fire. Shapes flicker in the flames, as if ghosts were devouring spiders and snakes. From the ashes of the man, twin dragons arise, intertwined with one another, they grasp at the suns as they ascend. The chaos is held in the palm of a hooded girl. She closes her fist and the smell of cinders fills Magpie's nostrils.

"Do you read me?" asked Wolf again.

"Nothing," Magpie snapped.

"Stand down. Operation Ba'al is a no go. A helicopter has been sent to pick you up."

"Understood."

A second of defiance, for a future of security. *Terror to prevent terror. Committed to the contradiction.* The words of S.E.L. Tactics used to end the war twenty-seven years ago. Ideals used to prevent further unrest. Actions lost because of cowardly governments.

Charles Jung

The audience whispers while the show is off air for yet another round of commercial breaks. Spotlights shine down on the centre stage, hiding the rest of the studio. Only gloomy figures can be made out in the background by the people watching at home. It feels as if it is a modern-day colosseum.

Makeup are touching up the host, a pale woman with beautiful western features. Once a small-time news reporter that used to do the fluff stories, now a major chat show host. She is playing very little mind to Charles who sits patiently for this all to be over.

Charles straightens his thick rimmed glasses and lets out a deep sigh.

Charles could be described as an unassuming man to those who don't know him. His blonde slicked back hair gives him a serious and yet unthreatening appearance. Due to his mother's influence, he is always dressed impeccably. Clean shaven and flawless skin, Charles' European heritage gives him defined handsome features.

All the chatter ends abruptly. The makeup artist quickly scurries off and around the studio camera men perk up. The hostess flicks her hair over her shoulders and sits back in the chair. Over the ear piece the producers give them the green light.

"Welcome back to all of you at home. Our next guest on the show is Dr Charles Jung. He is one of the greatest scientific minds of the century having solved the problem of terraforming at the age of twenty-one. I don't know about you guys, but I was up to all sorts of no good at twenty-one, not solving scientific quandaries. It is a pleasure to have you on the show. So, Charles, explain to the viewers at home a little bit about the history of terraforming and the myth of the 'Mars Question'," asked the hostess after an enthusiastic introduction.

Charles' eyes light up and in a perfectly composed temperament he begins to explain.

"Fifty years before the war, humankind was exploring the farthest reaches of our solar system. With major advancements made in space travel, for the first time in our history we could send manned voyages to study the most distant planets in our system. Our knowledge and understanding flourished, answering and opening questions about the mysteries of the universe. Once we reached the edge of our sun's immediate gravitational influence, scientists and pioneers began look to the stars beyond. That's when we began to experiment with Electromagnetic Relays, or EMRs if you will. Using electromagnetic technology to accelerate projectiles to enormous speeds, this allows for great distances between our solar system and other systems to be traversed within minimal time."

"So, light speed?" the hostess interrupted.

"Something like that," chuckled Charles. "The problem then arose; how do we stop the projectile once it reaches its destination? That's where Electromagnetic Nets come in, otherwise known as EMNs. These series of nets would gradually slow down the projectile until the final net which would bring the projectile to its original speed when entering the EMR. This allows travel between systems to happen with relative ease. These journeys between systems were dubbed 'trajectory shots', pilots would have to be constantly vigilant long the predicted line of trajectory, adjusting the craft mere points of degrees so not to miss the EMN target."

"So, what has this got to do with terraforming?" interrupted the hostess again.

"The original mission was to scout twenty planets that existed within the inhabitable zone with the aim to mediate their atmospheres so that we could eventually colonize them. This was based on numerous expert's research of Mars. Mars once had an atmosphere and with the confirmation that there was frozen water beneath the planet's surface and even the discovery of fungi, many then considered Mars a potentially viable planet. Attempts to jumpstart the planet's atmosphere was underway, however, limited success was ever made with Mars. That was until Professor Neil Harrison.

"Harrison took the lead in the field of terraforming and his research on Mars was deemed highly promising. Despite never succeeding in terraforming our neighbour, his research was duplicated on each of the twenty planets. Nine of which were successful. These planets became known as the 'First Nine'. The atmospheres were unstable and change was slow and arduous. Regardless, after the war the USA government insisted in colonizing the planets, endangering all those lives who were sent out there.

"During this time, I was a student at Oxford, my professor, none other than Harrison himself. He was a boastful man, littering his lectures with personal anecdotes of his time on Mars. What never sat well with me was that he was enjoying the riches of his research in a lecture hall down here on Earth, while his research and engineering teams where off planet trying to keep afloat a sinking ship."

"I sense some bad blood here Dr Jung," the hostess perked up, leading forward in her chair. "Please, do go on."

"As a student of his, I had direct access to his research. Very quickly I began to unravel its flaws. Ultimately, it was nonsense to assume terraforming would lead to homogenised environments and the fact that Mars was a failure meant his whole premise was fundamentally wrong. My behaviour as his student became increasingly hostile and more and more of my fellow cohort began questioning his research. Before I could submit my thesis, Harrison had arranged my expulsion from the university."

"If I am not mistaken, you also met your wife, Zhang Li, at university as well. Your wife is an interesting person, is she not?"

"By that you mean my wife is Chinese, yes," Charles said bluntly.

The audience murmur disapprovingly.

"A month after my expulsion a planet dubbed Delta Nine was experiencing catastrophic disasters," continued Charles, ignoring their prejudice. "Many of the scientists likened the red planet of Delta Nine to that of Mars, as it too is believed to have once supported its own atmosphere. However, it was always one of the more volatile planets colonised. The planet was rejecting the terraformed atmosphere. Hundreds died as result. Delta Nine was proof pre-existing ideas of terraforming were wrong and Harrison had no answers as to why it was happening. Bypassing the University, myself and my team travelled to the States to submit my thesis on terraforming to the American government itself. Within a week, we found ourselves on a ship travelling to Delta Nine with an expert team of engineers and generous funding."

"Why did you go out there too? Wasn't it dangerous?"

"Yes, but I insisted that I was to oversee every aspect of the construction. Besides, we did not have time to brief anyone on the ins and outs of the design. Once we got to Delta Nine, it was worse than any of us had expected. The colonists were suffering radiation poisoning and the acid rain had begun to eat away at the colony. It was the longest sixteen months of my life. People falling sick every day; food supplies spoiling; accidents because of sleep deprivation; and equipment degenerating due to the harsh conditions. Pockets of air low in oxygen would make the hard labour even more dangerous. The thunder at night would shake the very ground. Winds reaching up to a hundred miles per hour, destroying our previous day's work.

"I knew my Terraforming Plant would be violent in the first stage, so when we finally flipped the switch, for three months we were stationed underground. The only indication of what was happening outside were the sounds. Any monitoring equipment we had brought along was destroyed in the first few days. Because our bunker was attached to the Terraforming Plant, or the TFP, the structure would rattle and creek under the pressure of the forming atmosphere. But through the hardship, we became a sort of family. Putting on shows for one another, drinking and laughing. There wasn't really much else we could do at that stage," he said.

"So how did you know it was finally accomplished?" asked the hostess.

"The noises stopped one day and I took a walk outside," Charles smiled.

"Just like that?"

"Just like that."

"But that's not the end of the story, is it? It's no big secret that you are being summoned to the CERE tomorrow. Tell us what happened next Dr Jung," said the hostess.

"Certainly. The USA government was reluctant to recolonise Delta Nine after all that had happened. Which I suppose was understandable. I protested it was safe and managed to secure legal rights to Delta Nine's Terraforming Conditioning and Security, imposing certain sanctions and regulations that would ensure my TFP to only ever be intervened with direct permission from myself. Further it meant I held the rights to regulate the rate of colonisation and the fundamental technology and infrastructure of such colonies to ensure no strain would be placed on the environment. I secured those rights with support of the American government," explained Charles.

"This is where your wife's connections to the Independent Republic of Shanxi in China enabled you to colonise Delta Nine, was it not?"

"My wife is the daughter of Chairman Zhang Guozhi. During the war her father sheltered Chinese pacifists in a small community amongst the mountains of Shanxi. After the nuclear attacks that ended the war, this small community then declared independence from the remaining militant city states of Beijing and Shanghai. The community grew, with a focus on pre-Republic of China traditions and philosophies. They lived more earthly lives, providing for one another. But as it grew, more and more strain was put on them.

"I met my wife while at university. She had lived in Britain ever since she was a young girl, Chairman Zhang knew her life in China would be a harsh and brutal one. The next time she met her father, since the age of eight, was with me during our second year at Oxford. I'd paid for us to go out there. When we arrived in China, it was...desolate.

"I've been to the West Coast and seen what has become of LA, but it is not on the same scale as China. Men, women and children starving; the soil contaminated with radiation, unable to grow crops; most of the cattle are eaten or rotting out in the fields; buildings eroded away. The last remaining city states are at war with their own people, raping and pillaging. Slaughtering the weak and indoctrinating the strong. China may have launched the missiles first, but the total devastation that the US left the country in is unforgivable and so very unrecognised.

"I wanted to give these people a fresh chance. A new home. If the USA were unwilling to colonise Delta Nine with American colonists, they might approve the Chinese, and they did. Chairman Zhang lead a peaceful community looking to survive, so the USA appointed him as the head of the colony's assembly and the colony prospered despite the conditions on Delta Nine. A new city was erected in the place of the old one and because of the wealth of natural resources, individuals became affluent, enabling further construction and development of the colony. In honour of Chairman Zhang, the Council of the Elected Representatives of Earth renamed Delta Nine to Neo-Shanxi."

"There is no doubt that Neo-Shanxi has been a success and by the sounds of it has been largely commissioned by the CERE itself, but your influence doesn't stop there," said the hostess

A map of the Charted Systems is brought up in the glass floor below their feet. On people's television screens at home, it looks as if Charles and the hostess are celestial beings sitting above a galactic empire. The planet to be highlighted first is Earth, then Neo-Shanxi many systems away, then the remaining First Nine, and finally several new planets are highlighted. Each system is connected by their EMR lines of trajectory.

"So, we just saw the First Nine and here are the planets terraformed and colonised since. In the ten years since your success on Delta Nine, you were commissioned to terraform the other eight planets and managed to successfully terraform others, imposing your conditions and sanctions, which in turn allowed you to populate each of these colonies with large populations of Chinese and Asian colonists," she explained.

"All sanctioned by the American government and the CERE," interrupted Charles.

"Now you want to build a Terraforming Plant on Earth," said the hostess accusingly.

The audience gasps in disbelief.

"Is this true? And if so why?" she pressed.

Charles reaches over to the glass of water and takes small sips. His palms have become clammy and his tie feels tight around his neck, he is not sure if it is because of the heat from the lighting, the audience's glares or the nature of the questions. Slowly and gently he places his glass of water back down.

"Earth is dying…" Charles began.

The audience goes into a frenzy. Staff attempt to silence them, but the more the they are hushed, the louder they become. Charles plays chess often enough to realise he's been set up. The hostess was unknowing, her career isn't well enough established to have a man such as him on the show. He sits there disappointed; his optimism having been sorely misplaced.

The show cuts to another commercial break. Before anyone has given Charles the OK, he has removed his ear piece and is darting for the exit. Behind him the hostess fans herself, complaining to the producers about the heat.

One of the assistants is waiting for Charles at the exit with his coat. He throws it on and continues marching through the backstage.

The long-fitted black coat falls to just below his knees and the collar is high, reaching just above his nose. A thick lining is made to withstand the cold, radiation and acid rain. In built gloves and a hood are made of the same material. It was the same coat he wore twelve years ago when stepping out onto the surface of Delta Nine. A memento from his crowning achievement. The one material possession he has any love or true sentiment for. Designed by himself, the coat is one of many given to the rest of his team. If Charles learnt anything from his mother, image is everything and if anything is worth doing, it's worth doing in style.

Charles steps out of the studio and into the rain. While doing up his coat he looks across the street and attempts to read the worn-down billboard:

If you can read this, it means acid rain.
Stay indoors.

New York City, a mess of different skyscrapers from across the last few centuries, one of the most overcrowded cities in America, and far away from the West Coast and the nuclear fallout zones. The people here have no sense of community and are greedy and desperate. Some have lost their sense of humanity.

"Dr Jung," a voice called out.

Charles looks down the road to find an old man dress in an expensive Chinese suit holding an umbrella. The suit

57

has beautiful embroidery, over his left chest the embroidery meets to form the shape of a dragon's head. The dragon of the Neo-Shanxi Assembly.

"Chairman, what are you doing on Earth?" Charles called back as he walks to meet him.

Without saying anything, the Chairman wraps his arms around Charles and embraces him, making sure to keep the umbrella over his head. He pulls away and holds Charles in place.

"You look like you could do with a drink. Come, there is a local bar that allow Chinese," said Chairman Zhang sympathetically.

The bar is high-class, dimly lit, but most importantly tolerant of Chinese customers. The seats are red velvet and the fixtures and fittings are a dark rosewood. The lamp shades match the seats and have golden tassels. Behind the bar are spirits that date back before the war, a rarity in these times.

The men and women of the bar are finely dressed, many are Western businessmen with Asian mistresses. Seeing the Chairman and Charles walk in, every Asian customer brightens up. A waitress directs them to the best table in the bar overlooking a small lake. She explains that anything they order is on the house.

"*Thank you my dear. Xifeng for us,*" said Chairman Zhang in Chinese, slipping a generous tip into her hand.

The waitress acknowledges the gesture and shoots a look up at the CCTV camera. The red light, that indicates it is recording, switches off and the scientist and the politician can speak freely.

Zhang waits for the waitress to wander off back to the bar. "*I saw your interview...*"

"*I do not want to talk about it*," dismissed Charles quickly, also in Chinese.

"*Very well*," said Zhang while watching the rain fall over the lake. "*You know what is going to happen to you tomorrow, they will take everything from you*."

"*I do not get what it is they want to take from me. I made those planets viable, they commissioned all my regulations. They even were willing to gamble with the lives of thousands of Chinese*."

"*It was fine all the time they were unsure whether the terraforming would be successful or not, but now each colony is flourishing, new companies are finding traction and with the unlimited resources out there, day by day they are starting to rival even the most profitable conglomerates here on Earth. This planet is not only dying on an environmental level, but on an economic one too. Your regulations mean that powers here on Earth cannot establish themselves on the planets out there and therefore cannot compete. More people are signing up to colonisation programs every day. As more people leave Earth, the larger the colonies grow, the more they demand self-government. Neo-Shanxi is a shining example of stable and peaceful living. True democracy, something Earth gave up on before the war*," explained the Chairman.

"*I just wanted to make things better for people*," said Charles sincerely.

"*Excuse me*," the waitress intruded.

She places down a flask and two cups. After bowing she leaves the men in peace once again.

"*What you did for us was an act of kindness and compassion. You gave many innocent victims of war a second chance*," said Zhang, pouring them both a drink. "*That is why you are dangerous*."

"Kindness and compassion, dangerous?" reiterated Charles, slipping back into his native tongue.

"*After tomorrow, Earth will no longer be a safe place for you. If you lose they will want to apprehend your life's work, ensuring there is no piece of the puzzle that they do not own. With your research, they will not need you any longer. You will become nothing more than a voice they need to silence. If somehow you win the case, then within a month some accident will happen, there are dangerous divisions to Earth's governments that the public have no clue even exist,*" warned Zhang.

They both sip their drinks.

The rain was only the beginnings of a storm. The glass windows rattles, water collects in the road outside forming a stream and rubbish is blown into the air. Lightning strikes, illuminating the city. Thunder that follows causes the surface of their drinks to ripple.

Zhang points out to the lake over the road. "*You know New York never used to have a lake. It was formed because a bomb was dropped on the city during the war...*"

"*And once the war ended and the sky was scorched, the hole began to fill with acid rain. The water seeped into the soil and destroyed the greenery of Central Park. Over the years, the rain eroded the ground. Some of New York's oldest buildings began to collapse. People became homeless. Hundreds of people died of exposure,*" Charles finished the story.

"*No one was willing to house them, give them refuge.*"

They fall silent and sip their drinks again.

"*What do you suggest then?*" asked Charles, aware of the implications tomorrow's hearing may have.

"*Come with me to Neo-Shanxi,*" offered Zhang.

Charles laughs, choking on his drink.

"Charles I am serious. My daughter, my grandchild, my future grandchild. I will not sit by and see them in any form of danger. I have sacrificed too much in my life to ensure Li lives a good and safe life," said Zhang.

"Move to Shanxi, where rain eats through the metal frame of umbrellas, heat that melts the rubber of your boots and sandstorms that can last months. You think Shanxi will provide a safer existence for my wife and children than Earth?" chuckled Charles.

"You have not been there in years. Things are better now than they have ever been. We are growing cherry blossoms in the soil. The canyon is filling with water which we are purifying. Last winter we saw snow fall on the tops of the mountains. The Red Colony is now the crown jewel of the First Nine. Life on Shanxi would not be so bad for you. The people of Neo-Shanxi love you. For the rest of your life you would want for nothing. Your family would be treated with the respect and gratitude that they deserve. You would have a home in the Imperial Gardens. Young Alistair would have a good education, free from the prejudice my daughter had to endure. Charles, you could establish your own labs away from the restrictions of Earth. These people do not appreciate your genius. If they will not let you save Earth, help build Shanxi," said Zhang keeping eye contact with Charles all the while.

Charles looks out of the window across the street, the stream flooding over the sidewalk looks more like a river now, beyond the lake and at the city. The storm rages on and sirens can be heard in the distance.

"It is a generous offer, but Earth is my home. Despite how broken it may currently seem," he replied.

Zhang sighs, then finishes off his glass in one. He pours them both out another round from the flask.

"Sleep on it, the offer is always on the table. Come, let us drink. We should prepare for the hearing tomorrow. I hear that you are representing yourself. What madness drove you to such measures?"

Charles leans in and joked, *"Not madness, just sense on everyone else's behalf. No decent Western lawyer wanted to come near my case."*

Michael Hastings

"Hello Charles. Not that I don't love hearing from you, but you do realise it is three in the morning here in London? Hey, hey. Slow down…what is it you want me to do?" asked Michael, listening to a distressed and inebriated friend over the phone. "OK, so you want me to secure your research. Don't worry, I'll head right over."

Michael puts the phone down, rubs his eyes and lays there confused as he tries to figure out why Charles sounded so worried.

Waving his hand in front of the lamp, a dim light gently brightens the room. He sits up on the edge of the bed and begins to get dressed in the clothes he'd discarded onto to the floor only a few hours ago.

From the wardrobe, he finds his coat, identical to Charles', and straightens out the high collar as he marches through the hallway, grabbing his keys on the way out.

London is a silent and dark city at night. Frequent power outages keep the city on edge.

During the war, Britain's conglomerate government held off the advancement of the Russian Army from entering Western Europe. The government has secretly funded coups in the Middle East and Africa. Despite its influence and presence during the war, in the time of peace that followed the country could not sustain itself. Business thrived on the war economy and since plunging into austerity, the government's actions have become shady and steeped in conspiracy.

Armed police patrol the streets, ensuring anarchy does not erupt. Through fear and force, the country has remained stable. Worker's unions being disbanded and harsh curfews imposed on the population.

However, London, along with several other European cities, is recognised world over as one of the last beautiful cities on Earth.

When Michael arrives at the lobby of Charles' London apartment, neither the door man or night porter are there to greet him. He approaches the desk and looks over the counter to see a smashed coffee mug. Michael searches around again to see if anyone is there. No one in sight, he proceeds to the elevator.

Approaching the apartment door, he notices that the lock has been busted. Quietly he peers through the crack and finds at least five armed soldiers searching the place.

They're uniform does not belong to any country or mercenary group he knows of. The under layer is a black lightweight, skin-tight body suit. The midnight blue body armour strapped to the soldiers is enough to protect them, but allows for maximum movement. Each of them wear a tactical gas mask, the lenses are unusually large and have been blacked out. The soldiers resemble bugs more than they do humans. Most of the back of their heads are covered by the body suit, there is only one of the soldier's whose hair is on show. Written in sliver are the letters 'S.E.L.' and each soldier has a fabric band around their left arm, each with a different animal insignia.

The man with his hair on display has the most ambiguous insignia. It looks as if it were a mound of worms.

Michael clocks their guns, lightweight assault rifles equipped with a scope and silencer. An unfamiliar weapon.

"Sir, nothing to report," informed Worms to the person on the other end of his ear piece. He waits for a response. "Six rooms, Sir."

Michael perks up. Six rooms, it means they haven't found Charles' study.

Charles became paranoid after their success on Delta Nine when the US government persisted in buying his research from him. When Charles brought his London apartment, he alone redesigned the layout so that he could conceal his private study room.

Michael looks down the hall to a window. A lump in the back of his throat leaves him unable to breathe. His mind races as he tries to envision if the building has any form of ledge he might be able to shimmy along, while also calculating the probability of success and the dangers it could entail.

Silently and slowly he takes cautious steps towards the window. He lifts the latch and opens it, careful not to make a sound. His memory had not failed him and as he looks down, he finds a ledge that runs along the outside of the building.

"Fuck," Michael muttered under his breath.

This would not be the first-time Michael had to climb at a considerable height. Whilst working on the TFP on Delta Nine, him and Charles would have to scale the tower to make repairs or supervise construction.

Hanging half out of the window, Michael lowers one foot, probing about to find the ledge. As he lowers himself, he keeps his back straight and reaches his arm out across the wall to keep his balance. Prudently he begins to shimmy along.

With his back turned to the window, the soldier with the worms insignia is preoccupied with photos of Charles and Li. Michael decides now is as good of a moment to move than any other.

Making a brake for it, Worms catches Michael's reflection in the glass of the frame. Without hesitation, the soldier drops the photo, clutches his rifle, swings around and fires a round at the figure at the window.

Shock grips Michael as the bullet pierces his shoulder and shoots out the other side. He makes a reactionary decision and throws his body over, clearing the window. Facing the wall, he attempts to dig his fingers into the gaps between the brick.

Michael rests against the wall for a moment, his body feels as if it is swaying back and forth.

With no time to lose, he shakes his head and picks up the pace making his way to the study window.

"Keep searching," a soldier ordered from the apartment.

The window opens and Michael looks to see Worms peering out at him. Moving quicker towards the edge of the building Michael glances back again. This time Worms is perched on the ledge, hanging from the window. Though his face is hidden behind the mask, Michael senses the soldier grinning at him.

"It's a beautiful night," called Worms, his Australian accent penetrating through the muffling of the mask. "Ever since the war, you can't get nights like these back in Melbourne."

There is a pause as Worms appreciates the night sky. Through his mask, he takes a deep breath.

"Say, what ya doing all the way out there. Come back inside, maybe we could talk. Get that wound sorted out?"

Michael doesn't respond.

Worms gazes back out onto the city and Michael decides he should move. As he takes the next step, a shot is fired near his feet. Panicked, he scrambles farther along the ledge. Before he gets too far another shot is fired. This time bringing Michael to a stop. He looks back at Worms to see him with his rifle aimed right at him.

"I don't want this to get messy. I shoot you now, your body will fall to the ground below. We're up at a considerable distance, your body would just go splat. We'd wake up the whole dammed neighbourhood. Let's just keep it between you and me," said Worms.

"Well you know the strange thing is, I just live right around the corner," Michael mockingly joked with a croak in his voice.

Worms laughs at the foolhardiness of the remark. "Now don't go anywhere. I'll be back in a second."

He swings back indoors, calling out orders to his squad who are still searching the apartment. Michael decides this his opportunity to go for it.

Outside of Charles' study he searches about the inside of his coat sleeve to find the gloves hidden inside. The coat was made to withstand the toughest of environments, it was made to withstand the manual labour of working on the TFP. He puts his hand in the glove and punches through the glass.

"Hear that ladies. We seem to have a pest problem," Worms called through the wall of the study.

Michael brushes himself off and switches the old-fashioned lamp on by the electric plug socket. Charles always did have a taste for turn of the twenty first century appliances, a guilty pleasure despite the environmental cost.

The lamp reveals a finely decorated study, complete with books on physics, chemistry, environmental science, astronomy and engineering. Scattered across his desk are papers with equations and designs drawn on them, the likes even Michael hasn't ever seen. Chalk boards and pin boards detail more projects and theories. Charles is considered archaic in how he works, refusing to store much of his works digitally. He has a humble belief that honest work must be done with the hand. Personality defines science, both in its flaws and perfection.

Michael scans the room bemused, knowing what he is searching for, but unsure of where to find it.

Loud knocking startles Michael, as Worms begins to test the strength of the partition. It appears the soldier is not too concerned about finding the hidden entrance to the room. The knocking begins to interchange with bangs and thuds. Then singing.

"Up jumped the swagman and sprang into the billabong,
'You'll never catch me alive!' said he,
And his ghost may be heard as you pass by that billabong:
'You'll come a-waltzing Matilda, with me."

From outside the room, Michael can hear steps skipping away from the wall. He stands there frozen, waiting for what is going to happen next.

Then the voice begins again.

"Waltzing Matilda, waltzing Matilda,"

Worms charges. A foot slams against the wall.

"You'll come a-waltzing Matilda, with me,"

Another thud. Dust flies off the wall.

"And he sang as he watched and waited till his billy boiled:
'You'll come a-waltzing Matilda, with me.'"

Bullets are fired, penetrating the partition. Papers, books and ornaments begin to fly about the room as they are hit by indiscriminate bullets. Michael drops to the floor, holding his hands above his head.

After a minute of a continuous barrage of bullets, the room begins to settle. Michael pulls himself together again and hastily rummages through Charles's draws. By chance he finds a false bottom and within he finds a memory stick wrapped in masking tape marked '*Taiyi Shengshui*'.

Worm peers through the holes in the wall, watching Michael's every move.

"I see you."

Worms backs up and begins to kick again. Each blow weakens what separates Michael from them. Chunks of the wall begin to dislodge. It would only be a matter of seconds before the whole thing gives in.

Michael places the memory stick into his pocket, ensuring its safety. With nowhere else to escape, he returns to the window. Directly below is an overflowing bin to break his fall. Trying not to over think it, Michael climbs out and dangles himself from the ledge.

A loud crash startles Michael as the study wall is finally kicked in. Dust fills the room and the members of S.E.L. clamber through the hole. Worms quickly scans the room before looking out of the open window. Down below there is no sign of the man, having vanished into the darkness of London's streets.

Charles Jung

Dripping wet, Charles searches for his keys. The alcohol has gone to his head, but despite his condition, Charles remains considerate and tries his best not to wake Li or Alistair. He unlocks the apartment door and stumbles in.

The lights are dimmed and the TV still on. On the sofa lays Li, unstirred by his entrance. It is closing the door that wakes up his wife.

In her delirious state, she looks at her husband, then at the analogue clock hung on the wall, another remnant from an age long since passed.

"It's really late. And your soaking wet," said Li worried.

Charles hangs up his coat and joins Li on the sofa. He moves her hair out of her face.

"I'm sorry about that. Your father is on Earth."

"My father is on Earth? Why?" Li asked, the news shaking her out of her dream like state.

"I guess news travels far. The Chairman wanted to help with my case tomorrow. He offered a good Chinese lawyer," said Charles.

"Please tell me you refused."

"Of course. But he did offer us something different as well," continued Charles, cleaning his glasses. "He said that there is a home waiting for us on Shanxi. The

69

arrangements have been made. We would have a home in the Imperial Gardens. Our own labs."

Charles stops there and looks off into the distance, as if he were contemplating the proposal. Li sighs and pulls her husband in, kissing him firmly on the lips.

"Gardens on Shanxi?" she said amused and they both laugh at the absurdity. "The Chinese have no home. It is one thing for them to seek peace elsewhere, but we have Earth. Things aren't perfect, but if we left now, what good would it do?"

"I know, but…Neo-Shanxi began with us. If your father isn't exaggerating, then we could help it prosper and grow. Maybe we could still do some good, help the people who want it. Our children's lives would be better. For both Alistair and Oscar," Charles proposed to Li as he places his hand on her bump.

"Mmmmm…" deliberated Li out loud.

Slowly she sits up, using the arm of the sofa for support. Without looking, she waves the palm of her hand towards the TV screen and it switches off. She begins to unbutton Charles' waist coat.

"We should head to bed. We only have," she said, rolling up his sleeve to look at his watch, "five hours until you have to be up for the hearing."

Li's face changes as exhaustion settles in. Charles ignores her concern and leans in closer for another kiss.

*

Charles looks out the bedroom window onto the city while he does up his shirt buttons, estimating the damage last night's storm caused New York. Drops of rain, infused with a greenish tinge, run down the glass.

Li appears from behind, handing him a freshly made coffee. Wrapping her arms around his body, they watch the view together.

"I gave them the stars," Charles uttered, hoping Li couldn't hear his remark.

He takes a sip of the coffee to hide his embarrassment. Li tightens her arms around him.

"It's not what you gave them. It's what they do with that gift that matters. Have faith, they are not all blinded by profit. They will want to keep you around, as an adviser. They have no idea how the technology works. Turn around," Li instructed, measuring him up and ensures his collar is straight.

"I know. But I won't give it to them. I won't be second to him," said Charles.

Li tugs on his collar, shaking him out of his own head. She brings him in for a long kiss. As they break away he looks at her almost annoyed.

"Be flexible," she said, leaving him with a seductive smile as she goes to fetch a tie.

Charles returns to the view. "Not that tie. The next one to the right."

"Do you not trust me?"

"Not when it comes to fashion. I don't trust any woman other than my mother when it comes to what to wear," joked Charles.

Li picks out her choice regardless. She walks over to him, throws the tie over his head and begins to fix him up.

"You're such a mummy's boy. Trust me on this one," she jabbed.

The tie that she chose is the tie her father had made specially for Charles, on the day he set out for the journey to Delta Nine along with the first of the Chinese colonists. It is black with red embroidery that forms Shenlong. Perhaps a precursor to the dragon of the Neo-Shanxi Assembly. He had never worn the tie, considering his ethnic background to be disingenuous to the cultural significance of the design. Charles does not protest though, knowing the importance of him wearing it today.

"How are you getting to court?" asked Li.

Charles smiles unintentionally. "Your father actually."

"I have a feeling my father came here for you more that he came here for me."

"I'm sure he'll come and visit after the trial," reassured Charles.

Li looks back at him and they exchange a glance of understanding. Before either of them can reconcile the moment, Alistair begins to cry from the other room. She moans and heads towards the door.

"I haven't heard from Michael yet," he said to himself.

"Should you have?"

"Should have done," Charles whispered.

Down at the entrance of the building, Chairman Zhang is waiting for his son-in-law. Besides him stands a young muscular Chinese man holding an umbrella over both of their heads. Charles steps out from the building and another young man gets out from the car and rushes over to Charles with an umbrella. He silently thanks the young man and walks towards the Chairman. Neither of them say anything to one another, they just give one another a simple nod.

Charles climbs into the car.

"*You over there. You, come. Stay here. Look after my daughter,*" ordered Zhang to several of his men.

The car door opens and Zhang awkwardly climbs in, inelegantly enough to show his age. He takes his place next to Charles and indicates to the driver to go. The car pulls away and they sit in silence for the next few blocks.

"I am sorry to tell you Charles, this car runs off petroleum," said Zhang, looking to break the tension.

Charles looks at him as seriously as he can, then they break out in laughter.

Zhang pulls out a small photo from his inside pocket. He holds it in front of him for a while, long enough for Charles' interest to peek. The Chairman notices him staring and with a groan passes it over.

The photo is old and has rough edges, a sign of over handling and poor preservation. It is also slightly over exposed, washing the picture of its vibrancy. In the photo is a young Zhang, almost unrecognisable if it wasn't for the smile. Next to him is young woman that looks the splitting image of Li. Charles very quickly deduces who the young woman is. Behind them in the distance stands Edinburgh Castle.

Charles knows little about his father-in-law's life before the war. Li knows even less. Between them, neither could work out if he was once a business man, explaining his connection with the conglomerate governments of Britain; or a soldier, having fought in the conflicts of South Asia, a precursor to the war that would follow. Charles is too afraid to ask. All that matters, is who he is now.

Charles returns the photo and doesn't say anything at first. Then just as he finds the right words.

"She died during child birth. There were no doctors. No clean facilities. I did not know what I was doing. I had never delivered a baby. I had no idea about children," said Zhang. "I still do not."

"I...I'm so sorry," said Charles, not knowing what to say.

"Do not be, daft fool. I was sorry for years. It did not bring me anything. But I never hated Li for it. Not ever. The moment she was born, I saw her mother in her. It broke my heart when I sent her off to England. I did not know that she would make it across China, let alone Russia to England. The pain that I carry, is the pain that I could not be her father any longer. I would not get to see her grow into the woman she is today."

Charles faces forward, his eyes looking passed the driver and out onto the road ahead of them. He is cynical about his father-in-law's sentiment. Then a profound realisation hits him; softly, but deeply.

"You understand what it is that I am saying?" asked Zhang.

Before Charles can answer, they are interrupted by sudden ringing.

He pulls his phone out from his jacket pocket. It's Michael. Looking back and forth between Zhang and his phone, Charles struggles with his sense of decorum. The Chairman nods, as if to give his blessing to interrupt the conversation.

"Michael, do you have it?"

Zhang sits back quietly, pretending not to listen in. Quickly it becomes apparent that something is wrong. Reaching for his own phone, the Chairman begins typing away. Messaging his contacts in London.

"Fuck," Charles exclaimed.

"Tell him to meet my men on Fleet Street. They will get him to New York by tonight," instructed the Chairman.

Charles relays the message and hangs up.

He slumps his body forward, plunging his head into his hands. Distraught, Charles thanks the Chairman under his breath. Zhang places a hand on his back.

The car turns the block and the court is insight.

"Be strong. We are arriving," said Zhang.

The press swarm them as they pull up to the court. Police rush over to hold back the mob. Zhang's men step out to help secure the area. The rabble push and shove trying to get the first shot. Their yells are indiscriminate noise.

When the car door opens, flashing light blinds them both. Following the Chairman, Charles steps out into crowd. Taking deep breaths, he begins to make his way through the narrow clearing that the police have carved. A helicopter flies over head. But to Charles' surprise, it does not stay to observe the spectacle.

Heading straight for the hearing, Charles takes his place alone before the council. Laying out his paper work, he contemplates the futility of doing so.

In the gallery sits powerful individuals of the political and business worlds. All with their own vested interest. Zhang sits surrounded by his men. Out of place, but not out of sorts.

"All rise," a voice boomed.

Charles watches as the aged men and women of the CERE walk into the room, sitting in front of their respective flags; United States of America, Britain, the European Union, India, Japan, Australia, Israel, Egypt, South Africa and the Middle Eastern Pact. All of which fought against China during the war.

Amongst the representatives is Professor Harrison. Older and frailer than Charles ever remembered his lecturer being.

Li Jung

Marking the latest batch of papers from the third-year undergrads, Li monotonously flicks though yet another average submission on Nuclei. Wine used to make the task bearable, but such a remedy is problematic in her current situation.

Their association with the university began as a means to scout for the gifted and talented. But as the years have gone by, few students have ever shown much promise.

Refusing to ever publish their research, both Li and Charles are content in their roles. Each preferring the practical application of science than the qualifications that come with academia. Since Alistair, neither of them have had much time to visit the university. Gradually commitments are broken and hobbies are being lost, despite her best efforts.

Outside the wind howls, distracting her from the papers. The violence of the weather is reminiscent of when they landed on Delta Nine. She remembers gazing upon the oncoming sandstorm as they stepped off the boat. A sea of red approaching at such speed, they all had to run back in.

For a moment, she loses herself in the world she once inhabited. Then Alistair from down the hall begins to cry again. Li checks the time and concludes he must be hungry.

While walking down the hall, Alistair's cries begin to subside. Unsettled by the sudden silence, Li paces to the living room. Expecting to find her son in his playpen, she shaken at what she discovers.

"What a beautiful child," said the soldier in a French accent.

Her stunning auburn hair flows over a black military body suit and midnight blue armour. A cloth armband has an insignia of a magpie.

"I always like half breeds. They make the cutest babies."

Li watches the woman as she cradles her child. Maternal instinct takes over rational thought and Li attempts to move closer. Casually the soldier reaches for her pistol and places the barrel of the gun against Alistair's forehead. Li stops immediately.

"You know, I'll never be able to have children," said Magpie emotionlessly. "I think if I did have a child, I would want a boy. I would not want to name him anything fancy. I would want him to live an ordinary life, with a painfully ordinary name. Sounds funny, no?"

Li stands perfectly still, unable to move. Unable to respond.

Magpie walks towards the playpen and places Alistair back in. Her aim moves from the child to Li. The soldier scans the room, tilting her head at a slight angle. Mannerisms that don't seem completely human.

"I couldn't raise a child in New York though. Too much crime," Magpie said mockingly, beginning to meander around the room, inspecting random objects. "Wonder where you keep it?"

"Keep what?" Li foolishly asked.

"Taiyi Shengshui. I hope I didn't butcher the name. My Chinese is pretty poor," explained Magpie.

"It is not here."

A lengthy silence follows.

The soldier walks over to the window and stares at her own reflection. Her body suit seems to absorb the little sunlight shining through. A dark arura surrounds the woman.

Coming back from the errands Li had sent them on, her father's men meet at the bottom of the apartment building's stairs, both carrying a box of the same needless items. They remark on their frustration as they head up.

Magpie's ears twitch. Their conversation impossibly heard by the soldier. She moves over towards the front door. Li watches her confused, oblivious of what has put her so on edge.

"Do not move," threated Magpie.

The two of them wait. Gradually it becomes clear to Li as two voices speaking Chinese get closer and closer.

Magpie places her back against the wall, gripping her pistol with two hands. As the doorknob turns, the soldier raises her weapon.

Her father's men open the door wide and are just about to tell Li that she can't send them both on anymore errands, when they catch the look in her eyes. Before either of them can fully comprehend what is happening the door is slammed in their faces.

Forcing the door closed with her foot, Magpie begins to fire through the wood. Each shot is not as nearly as loud as Li had imagined, though each round is nerve rattling.

Several bullets find their way directly into one of the guard's chest. Blood spurts out, spraying the apartment. Retaliating, the other guard pulls out his gun and returns fire.

Gracefully, Magpie rolls out from behind the door, landing in a low stance. Ready to pounce. Her smile leaves him cold.

The force of her charge sends them flying out into the corridor.

Wrestling on the floor, Magpie overpowers him with ease. Pistol in hand, she begins to smash his face in. The first blow breaks his nose. The second loosens his teeth. The third almost blinds him.

Satisfied that he is spitting blood, she climbs to her feet and walks back into the apartment. Li watches the soldier's manic body language.

Her approach is cut short at the sound of gun fire. They both look down at the smoking hole in Magpie's abdomen.

Running on adrenaline, Magpie breaks for the stairs. Regaining his strength, her father's man picks himself up and gives chase. For every step he takes, she seems to have moved at least double.

Knowing he is be unable to catch her, he fires off a few rounds, nowhere close to hitting her. She leans over the banister laughing. Frustrated he continues the chase.

Proceeding cautiously, he sweeps the rooftop. At the edge of the building a black helicopter waits for Magpie. Placing pressure on her wound, she jumps on board. All he can do is watch as the helicopter begins to fly away. Magpie hangs herself out of the aircraft, casually saluting him as she escapes.

Charles Jung

Waiting out in the empty hall, Charles sits with his head in his hands. The first half of the hearing was tough. Much of it had seemed like mere formalities. He'd done the best he could to put across his case, though it felt like it mattered very little. The CERE have their own agenda, twisting every argument back towards Charles and his monopoly of control. For what he sees as prevention, the CERE see as an inherent threat. It is the first time he has begun to question the sanctions and regulations he imposed on the colonies.

Loud echoing footsteps approach Charles. Bring with him the smell of good coffee, the Chairman takes a seat on the bench. Charles sits up and takes the cup. They both take long sips.

"You did well in there. I am impressed. Perhaps there is a politician in you yet Charles," Zhang said in Chinese, hoping that it would make it harder for people to eavesdrop.

They both allow themselves to chuckle at the joke.

"Do not begin to question all the good that you have done for people."

Charles simply nods. The Chairman is left unsure if his words managed to reach him. But it does not matter, as Zhang has more important news to break to his son-in-law.

"There is something you need to know."

"Have your men manged to get to Michael?" Charles asked.

"Yes. But it is about Li," said the Chairman.

He lets Charles place his coffee down before continuing.

"She is fine. Both Li and Alistair are being moved to a secure location by my men as we speak."

"Tell me what happened."

"Li was attacked by a soldier looking for your research. It sounds as though it was the same group who were searching your apartment in London. One of my men was killed. Another brutally beaten. But they are safe and being taken to a safe place," he explained.

"Fuck," Charles exclaimed, unsure whether to scream or to cry. His leg taps involuntary.

"If they cannot get it through legal means, they will obtain it through violence. That is what they do. That is what they know."

The Chairman gives him a single but firm pat on the shoulder. Taking a loud sip of his coffee, he lets out a satisfied groan. The action seems to have distracted them both from their own thoughts.

Standing up, he waits for Charles to join him. "Are you ready to finish this?"

Zhang does not get a response.

"You are not a weak man. Do not behave as such now," he scolded.

Charles wipes away the tears gathering along the bottom of his eyelids and gets up. He fixes his glasses, then straightens his jacket. The Chairman proudly nods. From the other side of the hall a heavy door creeks open and a woman summons Charles back in.

"Please all be seated," the representative of the USA instructed the court. "Dr Charles Jung, thank you for your attendance today. We, the Council of the Elected Representatives of Earth, wanted to just commemorate you on your bravery today. Representing one's self is not a particularly easy task. You have done so with such earnest conviction. Before we continue, is there anything you would like to add?"

Charles stands, knowing whatever he says cannot change the outcome of the day. Glancing around the room, he quickly clears his throat. The press watch in anticipation. Chairman Zhang sits with his head held up high, meeting Charles' glaze with a reassuring smile.

Facing the CERE, Charles begins softly.

"We have forgotten basic truths about ourselves. Humanity is fragile. We exist by fortunate coincidence. Having evolved on a planet where the prefect conditions for life forever hang in the balance. At any time, those conditions could be snuffed out. By some cosmic coincidence. A global catastrophe. Or our own carelessness. Life on Earth has been erased many times over. The planet creating its own tabula rasa for new organisms to thrive. We have forgotten that accidents cost us so much. All that we do, all that I do, is only mere perversion if it were not for the betterment of humanity. Science knows no boarders. It does not differentiate between race.

"I arrived here today knowing that there could be no immediate resolution to our differences. Regardless, I know I have sown the seeds for change. Maybe not for my children, but perhaps for their children, or their children's children. As the most distant colonies acclimatise to life away from Earth, they will prosper. Eventually that prosperity will force Earth to adapt. Perhaps then we can have a more measured conversation. One that does not involve a backdrop of flags. Sensationalised media. Or the hatred borne of the past. When we can finally accept that we are one."

"Well said," the USA representative agreed. "Sentiments which I'm sure all of us here can relate to and hope for. As you yourself have just expressed, we seek further collaboration with you in the future. But that collaboration cannot be dictated by a single individual. We would all welcome your expertise as a key figure in the Ministry of Terraforming and Colonisation under Professor Neil Harrison. You would be given funding and an opportunity to share and develop your research.

"All previous regulations and sanctions on colonised planets will be lifted and will be henceforth monitored by the CERE. Already existing Assemblies will undergo evaluation and those remaining will be accountable to the CERE. Industries established on colonies will continue to be regulated to guarantee the stability of forming environments. Any corporation wanting to expand their business onto the colonies will be individually assessed and will have to compile with CERE regulations that shall be drawn up in negations with the Ministry of Terraforming and Colonisation. All pre-existing colonists will be given permanent citizenship and a constitution will be drawn up protecting their human rights."

With that the American slams the gavel down.

"All stand," called the bailiff in a loud authoritative voice.

The CERE and Harrison walk off. Charles has little care for his loss, all that he can think about is getting to Li and Alistair. Preoccupied by his own thoughts, he does not notice the volume erupting in the room. He is startled when a hand is placed on his back.

"We should leave," advised the Chairman.

Charles nods.

Exiting the courtroom, they are joined by several Chinese men in suits. They form a protective circle around Charles and Zhang. Pushing the press out of their way, they walk down through the hall towards the exit.

A plethora of questions bombard Charles. The camera lights blinding him. Microphone are invasively shoved in his face. Outside wait even more journalists.

Charles is unable to differentiate sound and visuals. All the voices meld into one. Faces dizzily race by.

The car door slams behind him. Lounging back into the seat, Charles is hit with fatigue. Not even having to be asked, the Chairman passes him a dose of aspirin and a glass bottle of water. Once he swallows the pills, Zhang give his driver the signal and they speed off down the street.

Before the Chairman can say anything to ease his pain, Charles interrupted, "Just take me to my wife and child."

*

"Finger print," the security officer demanded.

"Sure," replied the Chairman, placing his index finger on the scanner.

It takes a second for the system to load his data. The officer inspects the information thoroughly before giving him the all clear. Zhang walks through the gates to the airfield.

"Finger print."

Charles does as he is told.

"Why are you travelling with that chink? He your friend or something?" asked the officer quietly.

"Father-in-law actually," replied Charles.

The officer looks at him disgustedly before finally allowing him through. Re-joining the Chairman, they make their way to the two dual crafts waiting for them.

The matte grey boats, dubbed the Grey Heron, have been designed to traverse short distances through space and to fly in the atmosphere of a planet. They look ugly, but designed perfectly for both environments. Thrusters are not just located at the back; the front ones are used to decelerate and on either side, are rotational thrusters for adjusting navigation. Efficient is how the Grey Heron could best be described.

Standing around the boats are more of the Chairman's men, one with bloodstained clothes and a beaten face, Michael, and Li holding their child. The second they are in sight, Charles rushes over to embrace his wife.

Feeling an overwhelming sense of relief to see her husband safe, Li loses her strength. Alistair becomes heavy in her arms. Catching her, Charles holds them both tightly. Holding back her tears, she tries to explain what happened.

Charles glances over to Michael to find him with his arm in a sling.

"We are not safe here," said Charles. "Go with your father. I'll be along in a minute."

The Chairman offers to hold Alistair as they board the Grey Heron. Handing him over, Li steals a kiss from Charles before making her way to the boat.

The two friends are left to watch as the final preparations are made. Neither of them say anything for a long time.

Michael remembers the memory stick in his coat pocket. Holding it out in front of him, he is amused at how much trouble something so small could cause. Happy to rid himself of the danger, he places the stick into Charles' hand.

"You're not coming?"

"No," chuckled Michael.

"I will be back to settle things," reassured Charles. "I'm not just about to abandon everything we have here for Shanxi."

Michael dismisses the remark. "You have a family. People who depend on you. That is more important than anything left for you here. Focus on them first, I'll look after things here."

Charles places a hand over Michaels and holds it tight. No further words are shared between them. Neither of them want to bid farewell.

Walking to the Grey Heron, he passes the injured guard. Too horrified to make eye contact, Charles offers a nod of appreciation. From the boat appears the Chairman. He stands atop the stairs, beckoning Charles to join them.

Charles comes to a sudden stop. His legs unwilling to carry him any farther. Turning to face New York City, he stares out at a beautify chaotic sight. As the night descends, the pea green sky violently twists as another storm brews.

A black and white bird flies overhead distracting him from his thoughts.

"We had better get a move on if we want to avoid delays," called the Chairman.

"Right."

Everyone in their seats, the co-pilot goes around ensuring they are fastened in securely. He provides Li with ear muffs for Alistair to reduce the discomfort of climbing altitudes.

With the checks complete, he returns to his seat up front. The pilots both begin to flick switches and read meters. A button is pressed and the main lights inside the boat are replaced by a dim red glow. Loud clicks echo inside the hull. The two pilots begin to call out codes to one another.

Gradually the Grey Heron begins to tilt backwards. Ahead of the boat is a long track elevating them to a seventy-degree angle towards the sky. The electromagnetic rail sparks as it charges up.

There is no countdown. The only indication they are about to be launched at a high velocity into space is a buzzing.

Alistair erupts into screams that gargle in the back of his throat as the force of the acceleration bares down on them. The few teeth Charles has with fillings begin to feel like they could explode. All their ears pop at the same time.

It is only a matter of seconds for the green night sky to fade into blackness. The force that was baring down on them lifts, replaced by the sensation of falling.

Charles unbuckles his seatbelt. Already the Chairman is floating playfully around the boat. He grins joyfully like a child, summersaulting with no fear of injury.

Inviting Charles to join him in the cockpit, Zhang navigates the hull with no problems. Lifting himself from the seat, Charles bounces off the interior towards the front of the craft. He can't help but find delight in falling in zero gravity.

"Come, watch that spot," said the Chairman.

Charles uses the pilot's seat to steady himself. For a long time, it seems that they are staring at nothingness. Then a spec begins to take shape and that shape begins to increase in grandeur.

"There. The pride of Neo-Shanxi engineering."

"What is it?" Charles asked.

"The future of space travel. The largest carrier ship ever to be constructed. Too large to enter the atmosphere of a planet. Running on Laser Inertial Fusion Energy we can generate more power than any current ship. This not only allows prolonged periods out in space, perhaps indefinitely, but means it is the fastest ship known to human kind. In

eight months, we will be home on Neo-Shanxi," Zhang said excitedly.

The carrier ship is unlike anything Charles has ever seen. The main body is short. On each side are huge wings, that look more like shields, pointing diagonally outwards. Thrusters, that would dwarf their boat, are concealed in the wings. Though he body is small, it is the most elegantly deigned section of the ship. Charles is amazed by the sceptical. Such a feat of ingenuity is merely theoretical on Earth.

Feeling a tap on his ankle, he pulls Li towards the front of the boat. The moment she lays her eyes on the ship, she is lost for words. Both completely stunned.

"Only eight months? What do you call her?" Charles asked in disbelief.

The Chairman beams. *"The Cyclothone."*

THE FAMILY-PART ONE

Neo-Shanxi

Wesley Jung

The music playing over the speakers is an old classic C-pop song, remixed to give it a new lease of life. In the background of the track, the crackles can still be heard from when it was converted from wax. A novel sound that gives the bar a disingenuous sense of authenticity.

The whaling of the music competes with the boisterous conversations in the bar. An eclectic mix of people sit isolated from another. Western business men sit with their mistresses telling rude jokes whilst puffing on their e-cigarettes. Lone Chinese men and women sit at the bar slowly sipping on their drinks, some of them down and outs, many others scouting for potential clients. Rowdy groups of youths' cheer and shout from across the bar, occasionally leaving an awkward silence.

The floor is sticky with alcohol. Each step Wesley takes, it feels as if he is pealing his shoe off from what is made to look like wooden flooring. Everything in the bar is made to look like the real thing, but everyone knows it's mere imitation. If someone were ignorant enough to be oblivious to that fact upon initial impressions, they would soon find out with one taste of the liquor. Dwellings such as this are a far cry from the prestigious salons of the Political District.

The light glistens in the liquids displayed on the shelves and the incense burning fills the bar with a natural bajiao fragrance, another attempt to bring about authenticity.

Wesley takes a seat at the bar next to a Westerner and his mistress. He places down the used glasses and searches for the bartender. Over the other side of the bar a large order has been placed. Wesley slumps over and sorts out his sleeves while he waits.

His red cotton jacket hangs loose over a cream shirt. Donning the uniform of Chinese martial artists begun as a symbol of pride, over the years, the clothing became associated as a statement of defiance against CERE control and any Chinese youth that comply with the establishment.

Running down the right side of his face and neck is a tattoo of the Shanxi Dragon. The ink is still fresh. With his hair shaved at the back and sides, along with his stature, Wesley is an intimidating figure.

The bartender walks over to take Wesley's order, but the Westerner cuts across and interrupts.

"Sorry boy," the Westerner said to Wesley with contempt, then turned to the bartender, "could you turn down the music. I can't even hear myself think."

The bartender walks off to adjust the volume.

"*I am not your fucking boy, xiyang guizi,*" muttered Wesley, just as the music is lowered.

The man swivels around on his chair and stares Wesley down.

"*What did you just call me, boy?*" retorted the Westerner, trying to pronounce each word as best he can.

"*I called you a fucking xiyang guizi.*"

Having said his piece, Wesley signals to the bartender for more drinks.

The Westerner's face turns red and it takes a moment for the man to compose himself. Letting his temper subside, he continues the conversation with his companion for the evening.

"That is right, turn to your biǎozi. You destroy our country, take our home, take our women. Nothing to you is off limits," antagonised Wesley. *"You fucking biǎozi, letting a guizi put his jībā in you. What does it feel like when he is inside of you? Have you no shame?"*

The Westerner stands, towering over Wesley. His companion grabs his arm to pull him back. Taking a sip of his drink, Wesley listens while she pleads with the Westerner to leave the bar and find a table away from him.

Just as it seems like the Westerner is convinced, Wesley resumes hassling them.

"What do you call yourself? Because you are not Chinese any longer. If you think your Chinese, then come over to our table," he said while nodding his head in the direction of a small group of young males. *"I am sure we can make you remember what it feels like to be Chinese again."*

"You say one more thing and I will knock you flat," warned the Westerner.

Wesley steps down from the stool and squares up to the man. In comparison, Wesley is quite a bit shorter than him. The man realises just how young Wesley is.

"You are just a boy," dismissed the Westerner.

Something flips inside Wesley as the two of them walk away. Several people around the bar notice the sudden change in his body language, but none of them can react quick enough to stop Wesley shoving the man in the back.

Their drinks go flying and glass shatters all over the floor. His companion shrieks as the man is launched across the room, landing on a table.

Wesley pins the Westerner down and begins pommelling him with his fist.

93

Before Wesley's friends can join in, they are intercepted by a large group of Westerners.

Grabbing a glass bottle, Wesley holds it high above his head. Putting as much weight as he can behind the strike, he is taken by surprise when his arm does not follow through.

Glancing behind, he finds himself being held back by some of the other Westerners in the bar. Wesley resists the best he can, but gradually he is pulled away, taking five men to properly restrain him.

Held in place, he watches as the man is helped up from the table. His split lip gushing blood down his chin. From his jacket pocket, he pulls out a handkerchief to clean himself up.

The Westerner walks over to Wesley clutching his fist and he lands a punch square in his stomach. Having readied himself for the impact, Wesley stands there hunched over, laughing. His reaction invites another, landing just above the first.

A few more blows land in quick succession. Again, the stomach, then the chest and then the face.

The men holding Wesley jeer and snigger as he grows slightly heavier in their arms.

"Stop, stop. Do you not know who he is?" cried the companion.

"*Cào nǐ māde bī,*" insulted Wesley.

The man inspects the young troublemaker.

"I thought you looked a little light skinned," he scoffed. "Call the police. A night in the cells will sober him up."

The Westerner turns to his companion, takes her by the arm and heads for the exit. She glances back at Wesley, only for him to meet her gaze. She averts her eyes embarrassed.

"*Support Neo-Shanxi, exterminate the foreigners,*" shouted Wesley.

The other young Chinese in the bar cheer thunderously, the support for the radical slogan unsettles the Westerners. Nervous they all look to each other for reassurance.

The man with his companion stops at the door. He returns to Wesley, looming over him, and raises his fist high. Welcoming the strike, Wesley straightens his back, standing proud as the men behind him try to hold him in place.

Punched with full force, the taste of blood mixes with the alcohol.

*

Singing obnoxiously loud enough to keep the people in the other cells from sleeping, Wesley lays on the hard surface of the bench with his right hand chained to the wall. His nose bloody and his left eye black. The bottle of water that the police have provided for him stands on the floor untouched.

The cell is underground, it is cold and the white paint is beginning to show age.

"*I am waiting for you to return, I am waiting for you to return. I am dreaming of your return, I am dreaming of your return,*" sang Wesley.

"*Shut the fuck up,*" screamed the inmate in the next cell.

Other voices begin to scream down the corridor demanding him to stop. Ignoring everyone Wesley continues regardless.

An officer appears at his cell door and kicks the metal bars. *"Stop the singing."*

Wesley sits up and stares down the officer.

"And what will you do if I do not stop singing. Charge me for having a beautiful voice. Go sit back down, you know you cannot touch me," he said confrontationally.

The officer sheepishly returns to his desk, knowing full well he must be careful of how he behaves towards Wesley.

Laying back down, Wesley starts from the beginning of the song. This time even louder. The inmates rattle their cell doors in frustration.

In the early hours of the morning, a young man in a Chinese suit enters the police station. The embroidery of his jacket is beautiful and on the left chest it meets to form the head of a dragon. The dragon of the Shanxi Assembly.

The young man's hair is messy, reflecting the time of night rather than his usual upkeep. Clean shaven and boyishly handsome, his posture is one of importance and distinction.

The sergeant waits at the front desk for the young man. Upon his arrival, the two firmly shake hands. Both hide their familiarity, acknowledging the seriousness of their meeting.

"Good morning Mr Jung. Your brother is just downstairs in his usual cell. I will escort you down."

"Thank you," said Alistair.

The sergeant leads the way, more of a formality at this point. Everything in the station seems quiet. Doors closed. Whole offices sit in the dark. Walking through the station, it is clear they are working with a skeleton crew tonight.

"He was brought in looking pretty beat up. We refused any charges being pressed against him because of his

condition. But this is the fifth time in the last two months. That is not counting any of the times we have stopped him and his friends in the streets," explained the sergeant.

They approach a door with a light beaming through the cracks. The quiet of the station is interrupted by shouting and one lone voice singing.

Before opening the door, the sergeant turns to Alistair in a moment of sincerity.

"I have played the books as best I can, but there is only so long we can keep this up. Eventually your brother will do something that none of us can protect him from. Officials from the CERE are enquiring into our records. His name has come up a few times."

"I understand sergeant. It would be an embarrassment for my family, for your department and for the whole of Neo-Shanxi. But I have faith in my brother. At this stage I fear that it is all that I have," Alistair said diplomatically, showing only a little insight into his own thoughts.

The sergeant firmly pats Alistair on the shoulder, then opens the door.

The first thing to hit them is the light. They both squint until their eyes adjust. Then the smell hits them. The sergeant continues unfazed, but despite the many recent visits to the station, Alistair has not quite yet grown accustom to the smell of stale vomit and urine. He pulls out a handkerchief and holds it over his nose.

In each cell, Alistair is met with a desperate sight: stoned women with torn dresses laying undignified; passed out men, both Western and Chinese, sit in their own fluids. Most of the cells are full of drunks and opium addicts, occasionally they hold the odd thief or abusive male. But above all the whines, groans, screams and misery, is his brother singing to himself.

97

"I am waiting for you to return, I am waiting for you to return. I am dreaming of your return, I am dreaming of your return."

"Shut the fuck up!"

Then a loud thudding follows, as fists begin to beat against the wall.

"If you let me finish then I would not have to start from the beginning. Shit, maybe you could sing with me. Let us make a whole night of it," Wesley responded, pausing his song just to antagonise the inmates again.

A police officer emerges from a cell doing up his belt, he notices both his superior and Alistair approaching, then a woman walks out from the same cell doing up her dress. Not bothered by the two men, she makes her way to the exit. The officer stands ashamed of his actions.

Alistair watches as the sergeant scrutinises his officer. Disgusted, he pushes the officer into the cell and slams it closed. The other cells roar with amusement. The sergeant looks back at Alistair, neither of them wish to pursue the issue further.

Wesley stops singing as the door swings wide open and leans to his side, waiting to be un-cuffed.

As the sergeant frees him, he twists his arm to remind him of his place. Bearing the pain, Wesley knows he can do little to protest such treatment.

The sergeant wanders out of the cell to keep an eye on the other inmates.

Rubbing his freed wrist better, Wesley watches as Alistair squats down in front of him, neither of the brothers seem embarrassed by the situation.

For a long time, nothing is said.

"You know, I always did love Bai Guang," said Wesley inebriated. *"She was so stunning. I think my favourite*

movie is A Forgotten Woman. Makes me cry every single time."

Alistair merely nods.

"I have been waiting for you to return," chuckled Wesley.

"Let us go home brother," said Alistair softly.

"Only if you sing with me," insisted Wesley, imitating his brother's mannerisms. *"No one here knows the lyrics."*

"Shut the fuck up," yelled his neighbour.

Amusing only himself, Wesley continues to hum the tune.

Alistair places his arm around his brother and leads him out of the cell. The sergeant gives Alistair and long hard stare. They both know, regardless of the circumstances, this is the last time they would be seeing each other.

Outside the police station, the two brothers relish in the spectacle of the starry sky. Above the towering buildings, colours from distant suns create a tapestry of unparalleled splendour. For Wesley, it is the only sky he has ever known.

With little more than star light to guide their way through the sleeping streets of the Political District, they walk amongst buildings whose architectural majesty cannot be full recognised at such early hours. Together they follow the overhead train line to the nearest station. Alistair hopes that they are still running between districts.

"She died of colon cancer. What a way for a person to go out. Even the remarkable can die in an ordinary fashion," said Wesley.

"Why are you talking about Bai Guang so much?" asked Alistair.

"*Because I do not want the other conversation we are going to have right now,*" explained Wesley. "*You can be the big brother in the morning after breakfast.*"

They walk in silence for a while.

"*I am waiting for you to return,*" Alistair began singing.

The two brothers smile and then break out into song. They continue singing their way to the station.

*

The bedroom door is prudently opened, waking Wesley from his drunken slumber. Rolling over, he covers himself so that he appears decent.

Unembarrassed, as only young children are, a girl of no more than five walks in with a glass of water. The girl is dressed in an expensive red robe with golden floral embroidery. Her skin pale. Astonishingly dark brown eyes and long black hair.

Feeling worse for wear, Wesley turns over to look out the window. The morning sun is still yet to break. Stale alcohol wafts from his mouth making him feel slightly sick.

He beckons her over for a hug. She places down the water on the bedside cabinet and jumps into his arms.

"*Why are you up so early?*" Wesley asked, playfully growling.

"*It is time for breakfast. We always get up to have breakfast with father before he goes,*" explained the girl.

"*The sun is not even out. The night is for sleeping.*"

"*Uncle, you have to get up,*" she commanded.

She squirms out of the hug and goes to find him something suitable to wear. After rummaging about in the wardrobe for a while she returns to the bed with a set of clothes and a towel.

Resting them at the end of the bed, she smiles and explained with a sophistication beyond her age, "*The water in the bath is still warm. Breakfast will be in twenty minutes. Mother and Father will not be happy if you are not at the table in time.*"

"*Thank you, Jessica.*"

He waits for his niece to close the door behind her and as soon as it is shut, Wesley throws off the covers and reaches for the glass of water. Gulping it down, a trickle of water runs down his cheek, and with the last mouthful he swishes it around his mouth hoping to get rid of the horrid taste left from last night.

Dressed in only his underwear, he wraps the towel around himself and heads for the bathroom.

Wesley resents his brother for owning one of the most luxurious homes on Shanxi. The wooden flooring is genuine wood imported from Earth. Paintings, ornaments and ancient relics saved from China decorate the house. There is a warmth to his home that reminds Wesley of old images of life in China.

Underfloor heating makes every barefooted step inviting. Actual plants cleanse the air, not like the wax plants that are found almost everywhere else.

To even have a bathroom in the house is a sign of extravagance and privilege afforded only to those who live in the Imperial Gardens. But there is no wastage. The water will be used to wash the whole family, then it will be found a secondary use or recycled. Even in the Imperial Gardens, nothing is wasted.

Bathed and dressed, Wesley strolls down the hall to the dining room.

The rain cascades from the roof onto the patio. Gardeners are already busy making sure the flowers can survive this morning's weather. He waves just to acknowledge them, more than what he imagines Alistair does.

Wesley takes his place at the black lacquer dining table between Jessica and Nicholas.

With only a couple of years between them, it is obvious that Nicholas is the elder sibling. While his sister retains her childlike mischievous sensibilities, Nicholas is more wanting to adhere to the expectations and social situations of the adult world. Often this is misconstrued as an introverted shyness.

But Wesley knows better, nudging his nephew, they both share a smile.

Straightening the spoon and chop sticks so they are perfectly aligned, they wait patiently while Weishi, his brother's wife, finishes the breakfast in the kitchen.

"*Good morning brother,*" greeted Alistair pleasantly enough considering last night. "*Jessica, could you pour your uncle some tea.*"

She nods and leans over to the teapot in the centre of the table. Wesley watches as she expertly pours the dark golden liquid into a cup.

Distracting Jessica with a quick kiss placed upon her forehead, he takes the pot and refills her cup. Wesley then offers to pour Nicholas one, but he refuses unsure if it would be wrong of him to accept his uncle serving the household.

A gorgeous smell wafts in and Weishi rushes over to the table with breakfast. A large pot with a ladle sticking out is placed onto the food-warmer. Quickly she dashes back to fetch two plates which she lays down either side of the pot.

Jessica is just about to dive in first until Nicholas stops her haste. *"Uncle is our guest. You must wait until Father and Uncle have taken theirs."*

"Do not worry, you can take my place in the line," said Wesley.

Excitedly Jessica opens the pot and helps herself to a generous serving of congee, and then, to her brother's dismay, she takes the largest youtiao. Stopping at the third dish, she leans over carefully to inspect it. Jessica takes a huge sniff and tries to determine whether she would like it.

"It is good for you," encouraged her father as he scoops up a slice with his chopsticks and places it into his congee.

"Jessica do please sit back, allow your Uncle to help himself," insisted Weishi.

As she leans back onto her chair, two chopsticks dart passed her face and snatch a slice. Jessica watches her uncle as he places the whole thing into his mouth. Moaning in pleasure while he chews, he convinces her to try some.

Hesitantly she takes a bite. The saltiness of the fake meat leaves her very uncertain of the prospect of eating anymore.

"It is a lot better if you put it in your congee," explained her mother.

Wesley nods, confirming the advice.

There is a pause in conversation as everyone tucks into their breakfast. Words are replaced by the tapping of chopsticks and slurping.

Jessica pushed her fish substitute to one side of the bowl and buries it. Wesley winks to let her know she is secret safe with him.

Nicholas is the first to compliment his mother's food, everyone extends their gratitude afterwards.

"*What time are you meeting with Grandfather?*" Weishi asked her husband.

Alistair looks at his watch. "*Not long, maybe about ten minutes if I am lucky.*"

"*Wesley,*" she said, "*do you think you could look after Nicholas and Jessica today? Their nanny called in early this morning and she is too sick to work. It would not be any hassle. Lunch is already prepared and we would be back before dinner.*"

Wesley feels a kick from under the table and looks at Jessica trying to get his attention. He leans in close enough for her to whisper.

"*Mother is lying to you. I heard her on the phone telling Nanny not to come in today.*"

"*Jessica,*" scolded Alistair.

"*It is true,*" she protested.

Wesley mouths to his niece that he figured as much, reassuring her.

"*It would be a huge help if you could,*" added Alistair.

"*No problem. It will be fun,*" said Wesley, nodding to both of Alistair's children.

Even Nicholas seems to be pleased by the notion.

"*Wesley, you are a life saver,*" said Weishi.

A loud knocking comes from the front door. Alistair finishes his mouthful.

"*That will be the Chairman.*"

Tucking in his chair, Alistair rushes around from room to room, each time acquiring something different. First a jacket, then a coat, a briefcase, then an umbrella. The whole scenario looks well practiced. His wife and children wish him a good day and continue with their breakfast.

Before anyone else has an opportunity to claim the remainders of Alistair's breakfast, Jessica appears at her father's place and carries off the leftovers of his youtiao.

Alistair Jung

"*You cannot blame your brother for being angry,*" the Chairman counselled his grandson.

Unlike the early hours of the morning, the beauty of the Political District can now be fully appreciated. Each building unique. Patterned with rich vibrant colours. All distinctly based on old famous Chinese architecture.

The rain falls on to the city and is directed by the slight curvature of the pavements into the waterways either side. These open channels give the appearance that each structure has its own moat, small bridges connect the entrances to the street. Kept immaculately clean, the waterways carry rain down the channel to the nearest water plant. They serve as the arteries of the colony, ensuring its survival.

"*It is not that he is angry. It is that his anger is so directionless. Throwing punches at small time Western business men in seedy bars with a gang of thugs who are happy to sit back and watch him take the fault. It is an embarrassment. He spits in the face of you and our father,*" argued Alistair.

"*And what is it that you know of mine or your father's place here on Neo-Shanxi?*" chuckled Zhang. "*You were but babies when you and Oscar arrived on this planet. The colony was a hard place to live. Better than China granted, but hard regardless. The canyon that the city resides next to was once dry. You would not remember the summers when the droughts hit. Families would be found dead, rotting in their homes. It was Charles, your father, that changed the prospects of this colony. What these people owe to him, what they owe to me, is immeasurable. Do not count yourself or your brothers in either legacy.*

"*Talk of family honour is commendable,*" he continued, "*but it is your futures that you should be most concerned about. You should not frivolously worry about the reputation of a name, but the strength of your generation. If embarrassment is all that is at stake then be embarrassed. But it is more than humility that you will lose if your brother were to be deported to Earth. How do you expect to find strength if a part of you is missing?*"

Contemplating his grandfather's words, they continue through the crowded streets.

Business men and women weave in and out of one another hurrying to work. Teahouses open early to serve breakfast to those whose commute did not allow enough time to eat. The district's cleaners stand in the alleyways smoking waiting of the rush of people to subside.

The Shanxi Assembly is the second largest structure on the planet, after the TFP on the other side of the canyon, and dwarfs the other buildings of the city. A lasting relic of the first colonisation attempt of Delta Nine, it stands out as a botched visualisation of what society would look like away from Earth. Much of the building is made of glass and during autumn and spring, when the storms are at their worst, whole floors are closed off for safety reasons. Though still functioning as the colony's seat of power, it is a symbol of irony for many of the Chinese living on Neo-Shanxi.

Liang Huazhi Square, that the Assembly sits in the centre of, is the busiest area of the whole colony. Headquarters of major industry heavyweights, high end independent fashion retailers and extortionately priced restaurants serving imported meat, all fight for their place in the square.

"My grandson is a fool. But a fool that will be needed in the years to come," said Zhang, climbing the stairs to the Assembly. *"And you are right, he is directionless. It is our duty to nurture him. Just as it is our duty is to nurture all young Chinese who have lost what it means to be Chinese. It is our place as politicians to give purpose to those feelings, not for ourselves to be consumed by them."*

"And what purpose should we bestow onto my brother?"

Zhang smiled, *"I must first speak to your father before I can disclose such matters. But we must mind our words when we attend the Assembly. Certain whispers have been overheard concerning Wesley's antics last night. There are members of the CERE that would like to make an example of him. Whatever is said today, keep your emotions in check."*

"I understand Grandfather."

"Shall we go, the sharks are waiting for us," joked the Chairman.

The entrance hall of the Assembly building is grand. Walking in, Alistair and the Chairman are greeted with a huge golden statue of the Shanxi Dragon, the same dragon they wear on their chests. It's eyes wild. It's fangs sharp. The dragon sits atop a smooth boulder, sinking it's claws into the hard rock.

Behind is a waterfall, gently trickling down the rockery and into a pond that surrounds the dragon. There are lotus flowers and lily pads floating atop the water. Orange and creamy whites flicker in the pond, giving the illusion that there is organic life.

Deep, dark browns give the sense that the furnishings are made of wood. Marble stairs lead up behind the waterfall to the elevators.

On either side of the entrance are two front desks with staff working tirelessly. Despite the tranquil appearance of the hall, the atmosphere is frantic. Clerks, PA's, civil servants and politicians dart around completing their morning chores. A voice calls out to the Chairman as a young man rushes up to them, waving his tablet in the air.

"*Morning, Chairman. The Assembly is meeting in forty-five minutes.*"

The Chairman lets out a loud and abrasive laugh. "*I will barely have time for my morning tea. No doubt called by the CERE to catch us off guard,*" he said to Alistair.

"*Would you like me to circulate before the Assembly is called? See what I can find out,*" asked Alistair, making their way up the marble stairs.

"*There will be little need of that today. We cannot possibly learn more than what we are already expecting. If you could, arrange a conversation with Du Jianguo or one of the heads of the Shanxi Conservatives,*" requested the Chairman.

On the third to top floor, the members of the Shanxi Assembly wait to be called in.

The Whispering Circle, as it has become known as, forms a ring around the Assembly Hall. From this high up, the whole colony and its surrounding landscape can be seen. To the south is the canyon and the TFP, on sunny days, the reflection of the water's surface can just be made out from the deep depths. Stretching from the west to the north are mountains with thick layers of snow forming on the peaks. To the east is a wide-open red sand plane as far as the eye can see.

Politicians mingle in small groups, some partisan and others mixed. They gossip, collaborate, corroborate, share, trade and tease information while party spies wander the circle.

The Shanxi Chinese Representatives proudly display the Shanxi Dragon on their chests. By far they are the largest elected party of the Assembly.

The Shanxi Conservatives wear a golden Sanzuwu emblem and represent the more moderate interests of Chinese colonists.

The Shanxi Radicals are few, many having been removed of their position due to disruptive outbursts.

And finally, the CERE. Most of the members that comprise the party are individuals with varying business interests, the rest are directly appointed by the politicians of Earth. Unelected, their power is inflated by wealth, enterprise and protection from the constitutional amendments imposed following the Assembly's loss of independence.

"*Your grandchild summoned me,*" called out an old man, loud enough to be heard by all those around.

"*Du Jianguo, any louder and someone might hear you,*" the Chairman welcomed the politician wearing the golden three-legged crow.

Keeping his body language open, Zhang attempts to defuse interest from nearby spies. The manner in which he conducts himself has been practiced over years of playing the same game. His experience and level of deception far surpasses the rest of the Assembly's.

"*I hear my Grandson is to be the topic of conversation this morning?*"

Alistair stands beside the Chairman, watching intently. Learning from each gesture and each subtle pause. How his grandfather's posture straightens while being addressed.

"*I only hear what you hear Chairman. But you know what echoes through this circle is either frivolous scandal best fit for nothing more than drinks at Salon de Ning, or something to keep you sleepless at night*," said Du.

"*And so, is my Grandson frivolous gossip or something I should take heed of?*" asked the Chairman.

"*Sometimes gossip mutates into cautionary tales.*"

The two lean in close, whispering into one another's ear.

Alistair strains to hear the conversation, as he does so, he notices another eavesdropper from the group opposite them.

His grandfather pulls way deep in thought, or at least pretending to be.

"*I expect that the SCR can rely on the SC for support on this matter?*" asked Zhang.

Du sighed in uncertainty. "*We have given the SCR support over many issues throughout the years. There are many of my party that question if there is even a difference between us. There are those in the party who question my leadership because of that.*"

"*That is because despite our differences, we have a shared interest. To protect the next generation of Chinese and to allow them to flourish.*"

"I am not sure our decisions have led to a better life for our young people. These gangs in the Trading and Industrial Districts are a sign that perhaps we failed them. We should have integrated them into this changing culture, not promoted these martial arts clubs and cultural schemes," countered Du.

"Your concerns are mine. But you neglect the positive changes we have had; these young people want to fight because they truly believe that this colony is home. How many Chinese are fortunate enough to say they belong? This is my Grandchild we are talking about. He is the child of Charles Jung, the individual who offered you the gift of this planet. If we protect the wayward son today, I promise the Assembly will have conversations in the near future about what we can do to better integrate the youth."

Du sighs again.

"This may be the last time I can have everyone toe party line. It is because we are in debt to you, but there is only so much we can be expected to pay back," Du reluctantly conceded.

"Thank you, my dear friend. And in your debt, I am now," said Zhang. *"We should call the Assembly; enough time has been spent whispering."*

The Chairman and Alistair take their leave and head for the entrance to the Assembly Hall. Either side are two men and a gong. With only a nod, the gong is struck and the Whispering Circle falls silent. Each party begins to congregate behind the Chairman. First to enter is Zhang, followed by his party. The CERE are always last.

The Assembly Hall itself is a large circular room. Opposite the entrance is an elevated desk where the Chairman takes his seat. Everyone else takes a seat in the benches around the edge of the hall.

111

The Chairman slowly rises from his seat. *"Those who called this meeting, please stand."*

From the benches, Alistair watches the rest of the room intensely. Shocking even most of her party, Li He, the deputy leader of the Shanxi Conservatives stands. Directly behind her, Yao Hongwen, follows her example. On the far end of the room Israel Epstein, the head of the CERE here on Neo-Shanxi, joins his fellow conspirators.

"What is to be presented to the Assembly, Li He?" asked the Chairman.

"Chairman, we bring to the Assembly's attention what we believe to be a total disregard for the growth of civil disobedience and delinquent behaviour in certain youth groups in our city," she began.

Around Alistair, comments, quips and pre-emptive arguments are shared amongst the SCR party members. The SR farther down the bench are less subtle in their objections.

Li He continues reciting her prepared statement with conviction and confidence. Impressed, Alistair sits back with his tablet in hand, taking notes on both her argument and her aptitude for public speaking.

The Assembly settles in for a long session.

Oscar Jung

Buzz. Buzz.

Awoken by the intrusive nose of the intercom, Oscar's arm jerks out, knocking last night's half-drunk tea flying. The flask's lid pops off as it hits the ground and tea spills everywhere. Oscar swears profusely while gathering himself together after an uncomfortable sleep.

Persistently the intercom keeps sounding. With the little composure he can muster, he answers the call.

"*Yes?*"

"*Dr Jung is about to arrive. He is currently on the train over the canyon. I thought you would like to know,*" a colleague warned him.

Oscar looks across the room to a series of prototype military grade exoskeleton suits left out on display. For months, he has been tirelessly working to perfect the design.

Slim fitted, the black under layer consists of layers of microfibers that mimic human muscle and mossy green armour is strapped to venerable areas of the body. Resting on the table is the suit's helmet. A large orange visor covers the face, while the rest offers maximum protection. On the left chest is the familiar emblem of the Shanxi Dragon.

"*Thank you,*" Oscar said courteously. "*Could you send someone to clean up a spillage. And maybe order some breakfast from the canteen?*"

"*Yes, Mr Jung.*"

Oscar runs his fingers through his hair, roughing it up to make it look in some way presentable. Making sure his t-shirt is tucked in, he throws on his black and scarlet doubled layered blazer. Covering his prototypes under a sheet, he switches off the lights before rushing to meet his father.

The clinically white corridors of Jung Labs make it seem as if navigating through a labyrinth. With only the occasional coloured sign or sector number, even those who have worked here since it's construction lose their way around. It is the quirk that his father enjoys most about the facility.

Oscar reaches the entrance just as Charles walks through the door. Taking one look at his son, Charles passes by without saying a word. His coat flaps behind him as he maintains his pace.

"Good morning Father," said Oscar, catching up.

"You look a state," said Charles. "Another night spent sleeping at your desk. When was the last time you went home?"

Instead of thinking of a measured response, Oscar merely blows air through his closed lips. His father gives him a sharp look, which forces a response.

"I honestly can't remember."

Charles stops and turns to his son. "Do you even know where your son is?"

"Alexander should be at home with his nanny."

"No one has been at your apartment for the past few days. Xuan paid off the nanny and has taken Alexander," explained Charles.

"She is his mother," he argued.

"The point is that you have no clue where your child is," snapped Charles, appalled by his son's indifference.

Oscar looks around at his fellow colleagues, shuffling around awkwardly as they try their best not to take any notice.

"When people leave work tonight, I expect you to be on the train with them. Go home, have a shower, get a clean set of clothes, sleep in your own bed. And find your son," instructed Charles.

Not interested in any protest Oscar might put up, Charles leaves towards the direction of the TFP.

Uncomfortable in following his father in the same direction, he wanders off towards the canteen to find himself some breakfast and a fresh cup of tea.

By the afternoon, like most days, his father has returned to the city and Oscar can once again resume his own projects.

Funnelling a pipe cleaner down the barrel of a disassembled prototype, Oscar cleans up after what he hopes to be the last bit of tinkering he will have to do. Engraved on the side of the handguard are the characters *'Dragon Crescent'*.

Completely oblivious to the presence of his Grandfather standing by the door, it is only when he checks through the barrel does he see him.

"*Please excuse me, I did not wish to disturb you,*" apologised Zhang.

"*No trouble at all Grandfather, please come in. Take a seat. Let me clean myself up.*"

"*Please do not stand on any pomp or ceremony. Your work here is important, I am the one who has intruded upon your concentration,*" he said, inspecting his grandson's creations. "*I am pleased to see that everything is coming along suitably. That armour is most impressive.*"

"*Impressive yes. Financially feasible, not so much.*"

"*Cost should never be mentioned when talking about safeguarding lives. You worry about finishing it, I will worry about financing it. Besides there are many benefactors in Shanxi who have already pledged a considerable sum.*"

Oscar continues to clean the parts of the Dragon Crescent. "*I heard that there was a heated session today at the Assembly.*"

"*Bah!*" dismissed the Chairman. "*It is good to have a lively debate at times, keeps your mind sharp. Especially at this old age.*"

"*I cannot imagine Alistair was so untroubled by today.*"

"*Your older brother takes things too personally. But you already know this,*" said Zhang, leaning over his grandson's shoulder watching while he works.

"*It is not quite finished yet. There are still a few minor hitches to work out, but it is exactly what you asked for,*" said Oscar, pleased by the interest.

"*And more,*" Zhang said chuffed. "*Oscar, you have out done yourself. When do you think, it will be ready to put into production?*"

"*Optimistically a week. But that is dependent on my father. I have been instructed to go home at the end of the day.*"

"*That you must. It is important to look after your family. If we lose our family, we lose the very reason to fight. Come, you have done enough here for the day, accompany me back to the city. I can only spend so long in these labs until the lighting gives me a headache.*"

Oscar grabs a towel to wipe his hands. "*Yes, Grandfather.*"

Charles Jung

Strolling through the Imperial Gardens, Charles and Li find peace in the warmth of the evening sun. Shanxi has been good to them, better than it has been to so many others their age. Charles is just thankful that he still has a full head of hair.

A red sky covers the red planet. The moisture from the morning's torrential weather has already been absorbed by the soil, making it look as if it had been as glorious throughout the day.

Separated from the rest of the city by a cream wall, the Imperial Gardens feel miles away from the neighbouring Political and Industrial Districts. The quiet makes it feel as though they are closer to the mountains to the west then they are to the rest of the colony.

Vibrant flora blossom throughout the gardens. Pavilions out in the middle of ponds provide seclusion for the rich and poor alike. Trees and flowers are lovingly tended for by gardeners and botanists, they fulfil the painstaking duty left in the absence of birds and insects. Both Charles and Li have forgotten the chirps and rustling that wildlife brings to nature.

"Wonder what it would have been like if we had girls?" Charles thought to himself out loud.

Li bursts into laughter. "I don't think you could have handled girls."

"I suspect."

"They will be alright. They are still children. Remember it wasn't until thirty-four that we had Alistair. We'd lived life, made something of ourselves. Alistair and Weishi were only twenty-one when they had Nicholas. Life for Chinese is different on Shanxi. Such burdens are placed upon them. We give them so little time to grow and find themselves. Oscar and Wesley will come into their own, in their own time. We must have faith."

They cross over a small stream to find Li's father resting on a stone bench, admiring the view of the mountains. He pretends not to have noticed their presence.

Charles and Li glance at one another with the same look of fatigue. Keeping at their leisurely pace they approach the Chairman. He looks surprised to see them, as if their meeting were mere coincidence.

"Good evening. Is it not a magnificent view? I hope that I did not interrupt anything," said the Chairman.

"An evening stroll. Age catches up with you if you do not keep active," Li said jokingly.

"As if you two know anything about age yet. Wait until you get to my age, taking the time just to sit is pleasure enough," the Chairman ridiculed good naturedly.

"Let me guess, you would like to go for a drink?" Charles pre-empted his father-in-law.

*

A young beautiful girl and an older male counterpart sing from the stage of Salon de Ning. While she is flawless in every way, he sits on a stool with half a trouser leg rolled up to the stub where his leg once was. The contrast between the duo is a distinctly familiar sight on Shanxi.

The vermilion of the fabrics contrasts exquisitely with the Huanghuali furnishings. It is the most prestigious of all entertainment establishments within the city.

Around the Salon, waitresses and waiters keep the highest of standards as they serve each table, doing their best to be inconspicuous.

Sitting only tables apart, the most powerful members of the Neo-Shanxi Assembly and the most ruthless of Western businessmen enjoy the night's performance. Respectfully people watch with only a few silent conversations taking place.

Charles and Zhang are taken to a private booth with a perfect view of the stage. Wasting no time the waitress brings them over their orders, compliments of the house as per usual.

"*We should talk about your son,*" said Zhang quietly.

Charles wants to politely ignore the Chairman, but knows the futility of doing so.

"*He was brought up during the Shanxi Assembly today. If he is not careful, the CERE have every right to arrest him, then deport him. He will not be given a trial, just exiled to whatever remains of China.*"

"*My child is not of my creation. If I recall correctly, it was his grandfather that filled his head with tales of old China and the forgotten promise of a Chinese Delta-Nine,*" retorted Charles.

The Chairman scoffs at the remark and resigns to the initial defeat, leaning back into his seat to ponder over how to approach the matter.

They turn their attention to the stage as the duo finish singing. The crowd modestly applaud the performance. Blushing slightly, the two performers congratulate the band as well as one another. The young beautiful girl steps up to the microphone and the room falls silent.

"*Thank you,*" she began, "*you have been a wonderful audience tonight. We have a few more songs left this evening, but first I want to just take a break from singing and instead recite to you a poem.*

"*I first came across this poem when I was fifteen. Our headmistress took over our literary class and this was the first piece we were told to study. She taught us that the woman who wrote this was executed by a barbaric regime. But her death was in defiance of that regime.*

"While these words that I am about to read to you stayed with me throughout my life, I fear many of the young women in my class forgot them and now sell themselves for the pleasure of men. If you will allow me, Capping Rhymes with Sir Ishii from Sun's Root Land."

The young performer recites each line with such articulation that even those who are ill versed in Chinese poetry are captivated. Waiters and waitresses stop serving to listen. The quiver in her voice disappears as her nerves subside. Alone in the spotlight, she stands before the rich and powerful of Shanxi.

Upon finishing the last line, she stares out to room of bemused faces. Hoping to break the tension she leans into the microphone. *"Thank you."*

From the other side of the Salon, Zhang is the first to give a standing ovation. Taking a swig of his drink, Charles is no longer phased by the attention which his father-in-law brings on them.

A single tear runs down the Chairman's cheek. Wanting to dismiss the idiosyncrasies of an old man, the sentiment of the young girl's protest is too common for Charles to ignore. Scooting out from the booth, he joins Zhang in the applause.

The rest of the Chinese in the Salon are quick to follow their example.

"Thank you, thank you," blushed the girl.

A lull in the room allows for the band to begin playing their next song. Walking off to the wing, the girl leaves the stage for her partner's solo.

"Do you truly think Wesley is a product of my manipulation? Or do you think that these young people are angry? That they feel alienated. Their identity and home

has been taken from them," asked Zhang, sliding back into the booth.

"How do you suggest keeping my son out of trouble?"

"An old friend by the name of Sun Tzu came to Shanxi a few years ago. He was a hero to the independent Chinese still left on Earth, saving people from the Beijing and Shanghai Nationalist Forces. When Beijing struck a deal with CERE in exchange for his assassination, members of the SCR covertly agreed to offer him asylum in the colony. In return for his asylum he agreed to house some of our more outspoken youth," explained Zhang.

Just as Charles is about to enquire further into this man the SCR have been hiding away from the CERE, the young singer approaches their booth. Bowing, she waits for them to acknowledge her presence. Charles and the Chairman share a smile and make room for her.

"Hello, my child," Zhang greeted the young girl. *"Please join us."*

"Thank you, Chairman. I am honoured that you could see me tonight."

"Tell me, which is your passion, song or poetry? You are a gifted orator, as well as fortunate enough to have a golden voice," complemented the Chairman.

Taken back by his kind words, she explained, *"My headmistress was a wonderful woman. Empowering and a true intellect who had a passion for history and the arts. She passed on earlier this year. It was her who first taught me the strength that words could have. I believe regardless of how they are presented, it is just important that words are heard."*

"And tonight, I believe those words were indeed heard," said Zhang, nodding in agreement whilst looking at Charles.

"*What do you think is the future of your generation?*" asked Charles.

Shocked to be asked such a pessimistic question from the man who gave her generation their birthplace and home, the girl thinks over her response.

"*We are being exploited,*" she began in a measured manner. "*There are others who are clearly profiteering from our colony and yet we are powerless to resist. Our laws are not our own. Our culture is not our own. The words I spoke tonight are from a heritage that none of us can ever reconcile with. Despite their profundity, each line is merely stolen. Our lives are like raindrops that fall into the canyon. We are nothing more than a resource being used to build a better colony, priming the world for Westerners to come and snatch it from us. If we do not resist, we will be scorned by history.*"

The last few chords of the song are played and once again the audience claps. Her partner on stage cracks a few light-hearted jokes, ushering her to come back on.

Waving back embarrassed, she turns to Charles and Zhang. "*Excuse me.*"

Alone together, Zhang waits for Charles to continue the conversation, topping up their glasses.

Charles sighs. "*What does he do?*"

"*Runs a martial arts school in the Industrial District.*"

"*Military training. This is supposed to save my son from the CERE?*" questioned Charles.

"*It is a harmless group. He gives them discipline, focus...*" Zhang attempted to reassure his old friend.

"*Do not for a second think you can fool me,*" interrupted Charles.

Amused by the comment, Zhang holds his drink in the air toasting Charles' scepticism.

Charles leans back into his seat contemplating the words of the young girl. He wonders how many more like her there are. Whether his son's behaviour is a symptom of deeper tensions concealed from him behind the veil of generational division. Has his complacency made him conservative?

Already knowing he has convinced his son-in-law, Zhang turns his attention to the duo performing their last song of the evening.

Wesley Jung

The lights are flicked on.

Unsure of the time, he concludes that it must still be the early hours of the morning due to the sting of his eyes. Hiding under the covers, he tries his best to ignore this rude awakening.

"*Get up*," instructed Alistair.

"*What is the time*?"

"*Almost four*."

"*Why are you getting me up at four? Go back to bed yourself.*"

"*Put on some clothes and come to the dining room,*" he said, closing the door.

Feeling put out, Wesley does as he is told and finds out his clothes.

Wandering through the dark hall of Alistair's home, he heads for the dining room. The smell of breakfast wafts through the air. Suspicious of his brother's intent, Wesley treads carefully so to not make a sound. He peers through the crack of the door and scouts the room.

At the table with his brother is their grandfather. As if the Chairman had some hidden sense, he turns his head to meet Wesley's gaze. Swinging the door wide open, he sheepishly joins the two of them.

"*Why am I not surprised?*" said Wesley.

Alistair pours him some tea, which Wesley finds to be an odd act of kindness from his brother.

"*Thank you?*"

The Chairman inspects his grandson's face, blankly looking at the dragon crawling up from his neck.

"*Well you did say it was abrasive,*" Zhang said to Alistair.

Quickly Wesley realising what they are talking about and becomes defensive. "*That is none of your business. Why are you even here? It is so early in the morning.*"

He turns his head back and forth between the two of them, waiting for a straight answer. The Chairman in a calculated manner defers responsibility of offering an explanation by taking a sip of his tea.

"*Wesley, there is a problem. Yesterday at the Assembly the issue of extremist delinquent colonists was brought up by not only the head of the CERE, but by two senior members of SC. It was agreed that further conversations about introducing heavier penalties and sanctions would be discussed and decided upon in the next month or two. The current highest perpetrators would be subject to those new sanctions. Your name was on the list,*" Alistair explained calmly.

"*And you are just going to let them do that?*"

"*To a certain degree, it is out of our hands,*" admitted Alistair.

Outraged, Wesley stands up from his chair, sending it hurtling to ground.

"How can you let this happen? Are you not the fucking Chairman? What good is there in having an Assembly if politicians are willing to sell-out the Chinese in a heartbeat?" he argued, forgetting to control the volume of his voice.

"Hold your tongue child," snapped the Chairman.

The hot-headed youth is silenced. The look on their grandfather's face even sends a chill through Alistair.

A patter of footsteps comes down the hall. All three turn as the door opens and Jessica walks in rubbing the sleep from her eyes.

"Why are you fighting? Is Uncle Wesley in trouble?" she asked, confused at the presence of her father, uncle and great grandfather all wake and dressed.

Feeling guilty for his outburst, Wesley is about to comfort his niece, when Alistair steps in front of him and carries Jessica back out of the dining room. They listen as Alistair reassures her that everything is fine. Knowing he may be gone for some time, the two settle back down.

His grandfather waits for him to drink some of his tea before continuing. The floral fragrance sooths his temper.

"Forgive me Wesley," began Zhang, *"I forget that you three are not children any longer. We should talk as equals."*

"I just think that we are losing rights every single year. First, they closed the university, denying our brother his doctorate. Thankfully, because of our father, he was not forced to work in the factories. Now they want to target those who have limited enough prospects. Must we be subservient dogs to survive? What does it mean to be Chinese on Shanxi?"

Zhang nods in agreement. *"I completely understand. But anger is not a useful tool if the enemy is so deeply entrenched. Nor do I think complacency or faith that things will eventually get better are valid either. You would be surprised at how alike our concerns are. There are more like us. There are more that are like you. I can give you a place amongst our struggle, if you want it."*

Wesley finishes his tea.

"I have no interest in standing at your side in the Assembly. I not the same as my brother. Politics bores me."

"No, not the Assembly. If we are to secure Chinese prosperity then Shanxi needs an army."

*

The thick polluted morning mist of the Industrial District turns the sunrise a faint yellowish green, a sight more recognisable to those from Earth than those native to Shanxi. A circumstance that would have never of been allowed under Charles' environmental restrictions.

Offset from the splendour of its neighbouring districts, each street is lined with characterless factories and storehouses.

Leading the two brothers through the back streets, Chairman Zhang takes them to a small workshop in the very centre of the district. The door has been left unlocked and the three enter inside.

Cumbersome machinery sits static. Metal shavings litter the ground. There is a heat to the shop floor that only comes from hard labour. Ticking of a large clock hanging in the far end of the room fills the workshop.

Still unsure of where they are going, Wesley keeps close behind as they make their way through into the back and down a series of dark staircases. The deeper they descend below the colony, the colder it gets.

"One. Two. Three. One. Two. Three," yelled a harsh commanding voice.

Entering a large training hall, the three watch from the balcony whilst senior officers run through their morning drill. Men and women move to the rhythm of the instructor's calls. Upfront, he too participates in the routine.

Though not much younger than the Chairman, the instructor is fitter than any of the young officers before him. Shaved hair and darker skin than other Chinese on Shanxi, his body covered in scars.

Noticing they have guests, the instructor halts the drill. Showing both class and discipline every one of the officers stand to attention.

Climbing the stairs, the instructor rushes up to greet them.

"Good morning Chairman."

"Good morning. I would like to introduce to you my grandson, Wesley Jung. Wesley this is Sun Tzu."

Neither of them say anything.

Sun Tzu sizes up the youngest of the brothers, inspecting the dragon crawling up the side of his neck. Wanting to square up to the old soldier, Wesley is unnerved by a frenzied glint in his eye. He turns to Alistair, who gives him a reassuring nod. Wesley then knows there is no negotiation to be had.

Met with a crazed smile from Sun Tzu, the old man begins to chuckle to himself.

"You will be in Yong Squad," said Sun Tzu, then called out to the commanding officers below, *"Sun Ren, show Mr Jung to his quarters."*

"*Yes, Sir*," replied a female voice.

Stepping out of line, Sun Ren waits for her newest recruit to follow. Unconventionally and boyishly attractive, her features are accentuated by her hair shaved at the sides. Her sports bra shows off an old tattoo of carps leaping up a waterfall transcending into dragons. A tattoo that covers her entire back. One that she is now ashamed of.

"*The rest of you are dismissed. We reconvene at zero-eight-hundred hours*," announced Sun Tzu.

"*Wesley, I hope that you find purpose here. Sun Tzu is a good man and true to the prosperity of Chinese in the Charted Systems. Do what he says and you will pave the way for a better tomorrow for us all*," said his grandfather.

Alistair places a hand on Wesley's shoulder. "*Together we will build Shanxi so that one day it may stand on its own. Best of luck brother*."

"*Jung!*" called Sun Ren.

Wesley cannot think of the right words to say, still stunned at the sudden turn this morning has taken.

"*This way, quickly*," she ordered.

Astonished that a whole community has been living below everyone's feet, Wesley is taken through a maze of narrow corridors populated with young soldiers. Squad leaders yell out orders. Individuals run errands, while others complete their chores. No one is idol.

Sun Ren arrives at a door with '*Yong*' sprayed on it. Holding it open for him, Wesley is faced with a plain room with rows of beds running down either side and lockers at the back. Racing to the ends of their beds, the squad stand to attention.

"*We have a new addition to our squad. This is Wesley Jung of the Jung family. There will be no special privileges granted because of his family name,"* she called out, making sure he knows his place amongst his comrades. *"This is a proud squad, with zero disciplinary offences to its name. We are leading the competitions board and have no intension of losing that placement. We are the top squad because we follow five simple rules. Rule one."*

"You let one down, you let all down," the squad chanted back simultaneously.

"Rule two."

"Individuals die. Units survive."

"Rule three."

"Broken windows lead to broken limbs."

"Rule four."

"Sun Tzu is absolute."

"Rule five."

"Chinese we are, Chinese we will stay."

"Communal showers and facilities are down the corridor to the right. The mess hall is back the way we came and straight on. Breakfast is in half an hour. Your bed is at the far side. Personal belongings go in your locker at the end of the room. Your uniform is also kept in your locker. You have five minutes to change. Everyone must contribute, your responsibility will be mopping the corridors in the morning and washing dishes in the evening," she explained rigorously. *"Li Guang."*

"Fūrén," said a young gentle looking man, stepping out from the line.

"You are to ensure Jung knows the Neo-Shanxi Army's daily schedules," she ordered.

"Yes Fūrén."

With that she leaves the room and everyone relaxes. Wesley walks down towards his bed and is met by the men and women of his squad. There is something familiar about everyone in the room. Young, scarred and tattooed. Most pat him on the back as he walks by, others smile as if they know something he does not.

Disappointed at his measly personal space, he continues to find his locker. Already printed with his name, Wesley opens it to find four changes of clothes and a few essentials such as a toothbrush and razor. Checking the label in the trousers he is confused to find that they are the right fit.

"*The Chairman gave us your sizes a few days ago,*" explained Li Guang. "*Sun Ren runs a tight ship, but you would not want to be a part of any other squad. Get ready quickly, it is going to be a long day.*"

"*Where do I get changed?*"

"*Right here. Sorry there is not much privacy down here. You get used to it quickly. First time, we promise not to peek...too much.*"

Leaving him with a slap on the back, Wesley faces his locker and begins to unbutton his jacket. He does his best to undress as discreetly as possible, occasionally stopping to glace over his shoulder.

The moment he pulls his shirt over his head, a pair of hands grab the waist line of his trousers and yank them down to his ankles.

Cheers from his squad mates erupt, while a few girls in the dorm wolf whistle. Feeling his face turn red, Wesley throws off his shirt and drops to pull up his underwear.

Sneering back the squad, he sets his eyes on the nearest person laughing.

"*It is better to just get it over with. You will thank us when we strip down for our shower tonight,*" said Li above the noise.

From the streets of the Trading District, the towering buildings of the Political District can scarcely be seen. The closeness of the buildings make the district difficult to navigate at this time of night.

Business men walk with their arms interlinked with prostitutes and concubines, the sweet aroma of cheap Baijiu wafts through the air as Oscar passes them by. Groups of middle aged women dressed in expensive cheongsams sit outside bars playing mah-jong, cackling as they tell each other dirty jokes and recollect sexual encounters.

Every few yards vendors sell the best food in the city. The odd vendor chops up what looks like meat and if Oscar ever knew what cooked meat smelt like, he'd be able to know whether what they were cooking was the real thing.

But it's a scam. The price of the supposed meat dishes is extortionate, there to exploit the drunken night goers. Women of the night bait the Western business men to buy them their favourite dishes.

Each vendor specialises in different cuisine. The deep warmth of the spices of the Sichuan vendor; to the rich vinegar of the Shan vendor; to the subtler blend of herbs from the Hui vendor.

With the clash of languages, lights from the overhead lanterns and contrasting flavours in the air, the whole district is a sensory overload.

Hung outside one of the night clubs is a poster of his wife when she was younger, from a time before they had even met. Oscar is momentarily hurt when he sees that she is not using the 'Jung' name for tonight's performance.

As he enters the club, the bouncer stands up from his stool. Realising who it is, he takes back his seat and pulls out a carton of cigarettes. He holds them out for Oscar, but is politely refused.

"*She is currently on. Her set should be over soon,*" informed the bouncer.

"*Is there a kid with her?*"

"*Yeah. He is backstage in the dressing rooms.*"

Red velvet curtains and the sound of music guide him through to the main room.

Pitch black, with exception of the stage and bar, Oscar skirts around the edge of the room to buy a drink. Taking a seat on a stool, the bartender without saying a word rests a glass on a napkin and begins to pour Oscar a drink.

Xuan stands centre stage. Oscar's heart skips a beat, feeling just has he did the first time he saw her. She leans in ever so slightly and begins to sing into the ring-and-spring microphone.

Up in front of everyone, Xuan looks content. Her eyes smile. Always dressed in the finest satins available on Shanxi, she would not dare to be seen in anything less. Her hair beautifully pinned back, glistening in the light. Her make-up brings enough colour to her skin to hide how sickly pale she is. Oscar is concerned by how thin she appears.

Xuan sings the last line, spotting Oscar at the bar. Her initial unease is washed away by the applause. Blowing kisses, she laps up the admiration of the audience and walks off stage.

The band begin to play and the whole venue brakes out into conversation as they head towards the bar. Finishing his drink, Oscar leaves and heads for the '*Staff only*' door.

Oscar walks through the back of the club unchallenged by the staff, most are too busy to even notice him, others simply pretend he isn't there. Catching the smell of opium, he follows it down the hall to a dressing room. From outside he hears his son's voice.

"Hu, Hu, Hu!" Alexander cried in joy.

"Not again," said a woman disappointedly. *"You are too smart for me to play with you anymore. I need to take you to the tables at Ning."*

The woman playing cards with Alexander is startled by Oscar's sudden presence. She quickly finds composure and stares directly back.

For a moment, Oscar is certain he is going to have an argument on his hands. He studies the woman's face. Her cheeks are full, giving her face a circular appearance. She looks as if she has money, but Oscar already knows how she earns such a living.

"Child, collect your things and we will wait for your father outside," said the woman to his surprise.

Alexander, happy to see his father, holds up a bag full of sweets. *"Look at what I won from Madame. She is not very good at cards."*

His son's comment breaks the tension between the two of them. She laughs at herself as she gathers her things. Kneeling besides Alexander, Oscar helps pack away the cards.

Oscar picks up the last few cards and holds them out with a comforting smile.

"When will we see mother again?" asked Alexander.

"Soon. Mother just needs some time to get better," he said.

Alexander's face drops, any sense of happiness he had in that moment is lost.

"*Is mother sick? She should come home so we can look after her.*"

"*In time. Now go, wait outside for me.*"

With his well earnt bag of sweets in hand, Alexander is taken out of the dressing room by the woman. Oscar watches as the door closes behind them.

Behind the curtain a silhouetted figure sits slumped over a dresser. Already he can hear the deep quivering breath of his wife trying to hold back her tears.

Drawing the curtain back, Oscar is met with a sad sight of the room having been converted into an opium den. A half-naked young woman squirms about stoned on a bed of cushions, next to her sits a lamp and pipe. Though the woman gazes directly at Oscar, she does not see him.

His throat becomes tight and he finds it hard to breathe. Knowing what to have expected, he cannot help but be overcome by a sense of hopelessness.

Xuan sits to his right, her head in her hands and trembling in mortification. Oscar is conflicted, both furious and pitying her. Glancing back over to the half-naked stoned girl, Oscar finds his conviction.

"*You are taking him away again?*" asked Xuan, raising her head to look at her husband in the reflection of the mirror. Tears carry mascara down her cheeks.

A croak in the back of his throat upsets the rhythm of his words. "*Do you really think you are fit enough to look after our child?*"

"*At least I have time to look after him. That I love him enough to spend time with him.*"

"*How could you let our son be in a place like this? If you loved him you would clean up and come home.*"

"*Do you even still love me?*" asked Xuan in the mirror.

"*We met so young,*" Oscar replied vaguely, taken back by the question.

"*We were happy once, were we not?*"

"*Yeah. I think we were happy once. But we could not keep drinking and partying. We were an embarrassment to the family,*" said Oscar honestly.

"*Fuck your family,*" screamed Xuan, spinning around to launch a bottle of perfume at her husband.

It skims Oscar's ear, shattering into tiny shards against the wall behind. The stoned girl is barely fazed by the commotion.

Xuan throws herself at Oscar and begins beating him. Gradually losing strength, she falls into his arms.

"*Fuck your family.*"

Resting his head against hers, Oscar waits for Xuan to exhaust herself.

"*I thought I was so lucky. That is what all the girls would tell me. The Jung child prodigy was in love with me. How childish it was of me to ever think our love could be so simple. I believed that marrying a Jung would ensure my happiness for life. If only I knew how miserable we would make one another. It is a fruitless question, is it not? Do you still love me? It is the family name that must be kept from scandal and dishonour. Alexander is all that I live for now. To make sure he is happy and that one day he can escape your Grandfather's shadow.*"

Xuan stands up straight.

"*Do you still love me?*"

Oscar thinks over his response.

"*Alexander would like for you to come home. Clean yourself up and we will always welcome you back.*"

Her husband's words cut deep. The avoidance of the question is enough to confirm Xuan's thoughts.

Letting her go, Oscar leaves her. The door quietly closes behind him and Xuan falls to her knees. Weakened by the encounter, she does not have the energy left to even cry.

Wesley Jung

Rowdy screams and cheers come from the side of the ring as Wesley lands another punch. Still angry about the events of the morning, he proves his worth to the rest of his squad. His fists wrapped in tape. Sweat running down his shirtless back. His dragon on full display. He has already beaten two opponents.

Bouncing around the ring, he allows the adrenaline to dictate his reflexes. Everyone watching is surprised at the endurance and power of the young man who came from privilege.

Another swing comes sweeping across his face. Leaning backwards, already Wesley is executing his counterattack. Closing the gap between them, he hurls his knee into his opponent's lower chest.

Stumbling back winded, Wesley leaves them no opportunity to regain their composure and floors them with a single punch.

Tapping out, the crowd cheer on Wesley. Several members of the contender's squad drag them out of the ring. Sun Ren even seems to be impressed, conservatively clapping along.

"*Come on!*" cried Wesley. "*Come on.*"

But no one jumps into the ring.

Walking around the parameter, he tries to make eye contact with any potential fight. Turning to Sun Ren, he shrugs his shoulders playfully, disappointed at the lack of challengers.

The soldiers go silent and Sun Ren draws his attention behind him. Entering the ring is Sun Tzu. He undoes his shirt and throws it to one of his men in the crowd.

Sun Tzu stands ready, waiting for Wesley to accept his challenge.

"*Fuck, I cannot hit an old man*," Wesley said mockingly.

"*Then you forfeit?*" asked Sun Tzu.

Unwilling to concede, Wesley raises his fists. For a minute, neither of them move.

Impatient, Wesley makes the first move.

Before he can land his punch, Sun Tzu's knee is already in the side of his ribcage. Stunned by the speed and power of the strike he stumbles to the floor. One blow from the old man has knocked him off balance.

Sensing the next strike Wesley rolls out of the way. A thud lands where he just was. Climbing to his feet, Sun Tzu's next kick is already there to greet him.

Sent flying across the ring, he notices that the old man is holding his hands behind his back. Insulted, Wesley acts rashly. Back on his feet he charges at Sun Tzu, only to be kicked in the face. Blood splatters those in the front row.

Undeterred by the pain, Wesley wildly throws punches at the old man, each one being casually blocked.

Gabbing Wesley's arm, Sun Tzu draws him into his elbow and Wesley wheezes a sickly cough. Looking up at Sun Tzu, he finds a calm and collected man. A far cry from the crazed manic look of this morning.

Holding him in place, Wesley is unable to pull away from the elbow causing him increasing discomfort. Using his feet to try and sweep Sun Tzu onto the floor, Wesley cannot muster the strength to even move him an inch.

Bored of his feeble attempts, Sun Tzu draws his head back and then head-butts Wesley squarely on the nose. Blood bursts down his face as his nose is broken.

Still held in place, Wesley is unable to fall to the ground.

"*Do you forfeit?*"

"*Fuck you*," Wesley retorted without thinking.

Another blow to his stomach leaves him limp, but still unable to fall.

"*Forfeit.*"

"*No*," Wesley spat in his face.

Wesley's centre of gravity shifts as he is brought over the shoulder of the old man and thrown down onto the ring.

"*Forfeit.*"

"No," screamed Wesley, slipping into English.

Sun Tzu manoeuvres over his body, twisting his arm, feeling as if it could be pulled from the socket at any time.

"*Are you Chinese?*" Sun Tzu questioned.

"*Fuck you.*"

"*Are you Chinese?*"

"*Yes!*"

Sun Tzu lets go of his arm. "*Then prove it.*"

*

In the co-ed showers, soldiers joke and laugh over previous fights or foolish things they once got up to. Wesley leans against the shower watching the blood run down his naked body, mixing with the water as it is carried off down the drain.

"*You should get that seen to*," said Sun Ren.

"*Yes, Fūrén,*" complied Wesley, noticing how unbothered she is by her own nudity.

"*You are not the only one he has beaten like that,*" she sympathised, knowing that was probably the first-time Wesley's pride has been crushed.

She turns around and shows him a mark that has never healed under her ribs.

"*This was given to me on my first evening here. I thought I could take him on too. But it was a valuable lesson and one that I am thankful for.*"

Wesley nods in appreciation.

"*Get that seen to. Go to bed, get some sleep. I will see you bright and early tomorrow,*" she ordered. "*Welcome to the Neo-Shanxi Army.*"

Watching as she leaves, Wesley studies Sun Ren's tattoo. Each carp fighting against the cascading water. Just as she had once believed herself to be a dragon, Wesley regrets the dragon on his own skin.

The water switches off and the showers begin to empty. Feeling the last drops splash against his skin, he contemplates the lesson he has been taught tonight.

*

Awake in bed, Wesley tosses and turns. The bandage over his nose is warm and uncomfortable. His mind races, flicking through thoughts of the fight. The speed in which Sun Tzu moved. The perfection of his technique.

Resigning to a sleepless night, he decides he needs some fresh air. Quietly getting out of bed, he throws on some clothes and heads out into the narrow corridors of the underground facility.

Everything is still. The thick concrete walls keep his nightly stroll undetected.

Having taken a wrong turn somewhere, Wesley stumbles across an open room with its lights still on. Incense burns, soothing the stale air.

Inside Sun Tzu practices with a Jian. His movements are precise and graceful, almost as if he were dancing with the sword, seamlessly flowing from stance to stance.

Sensing that Wesley is by the door he stops. Sheathing the sword Sun Tzu waits for Wesley to start the conversation.

"*Why do you practice with a sword? I cannot imagine it would have been much use to you in China*," asked Wesley.

"*It is a state of mind over anything else. There is a reason why I survived and others fell. There is a reason why you were beaten tonight*," he explained.

"*And you can learn that from swinging some sword?*"

Sun Tzu laughs. "*No. Not from swinging some sword. But learning balance. Finding clarity in your movements. By clearing your mind.*"

Wesley approaches the old man, standing at his side.

"*What was it like in China? Grandfather only tells me about some great nation with a complicated but grand history. What was it really like after the war?*"

"*I was twenty-one when the war began,*" Sun Tzu started, "*only a little older than yourself. The men of Weifang were amongst the first to be forcefully conscripted. They came for us during the night. We were dragged out into the streets and loaded up onto trucks. Mothers, wives, sisters and daughters stood helpless as we were driven away.*

"*Before I knew it, I was on the front lines, part of the push to eliminate Western forces from Zhejiang. I had* never once imagined myself as a soldier. I was angry at the injustice our government had committed. But when I was there I realised why they needed us. Men and women in mass were thrown at the enemy. Wave after wave, torn to shreds. Bits of people scattered the battlefield. The best some soldiers could do was throw themselves at the bipedal tanks with explosives strapped to them. Dare to Die Squads.

"After one battle, I found myself buried under a pile of corpses. For two days, I was left there. The rotting flesh and the excrement seeping down to where I lay. When they found me, I was cleaned up and sent out to fight again.

"I was stationed all over China. Towards the end, we were sent to Japan. I was there when Osaka fell. When the Chairman was assassinated my unit was in Shanghai. We watched as the missiles flew overhead and ignited the sky.

"The war was lost. The government overthrown. In its place a provisional government just as war hungry as the last. Destressing news came from Datong of soldiers massacring civilians and the country became fragmented. Civil unrest swept across China as the people rebelled against the new government, Beijing and Shanghai tried to maintain order.

"Again, I was conscripted into the army. This time into the Shanghai Peace Militia. The Nationalist Forces had some questionable divisions, none so questionable than the Peace Militia. Public executions, torture and the extermination of whole rebel villages.

"That is when I first met your grandfather. My squad were ordered to neutralise a growing separatist community in the mountains of Shanxi. But he gave us a choice. Live as dogs, or die like heroes. Death had never *crossed my mind as being an honourable thing. I had seen war. I had seen death. There was no honour for those men and women who has lost their lives.*

"But guilt had consumed us for long enough. We stayed to protect Zhang Guozhi and his community. It was in those mountains that I studied the sword. Learnt what it meant to belong. What it meant to be Chinese. After two years, I decided to go back east and help my fellow countrymen escape the tyranny of the Nationalist Forces.

"Years passed. Stories of Zhang Guozhi and his peaceful community in the mountains of Shanxi would reach me. I would take solace knowing all those I saved were safe. Then one day the stories stopped.

"When I returned, the mountains were all but abandoned. Those few left told me of Dr Charles Jung and the Chinese colony of Delta-Nine, a new home for the Chinese to begin again. I knew then it was my duty to continue saving people from the clutches of the Beijing and Shanghai Nationalists.

"Both the Nationalists and Western governments saw me as a threat. They tried their hardest to take me out. As I grew older, the closer they came to succeeding. One day, a man in a suit found me injured in the backstreets of Nanjing. He told me that Chairman Zhang wanted me to join his colony and help build a better future for its younger generation. We have been preparing ever since," finished Sun Tzu.

Wesley tries to fully comprehend all that he has been told.

"Is that why you are not asleep?"

"I have not slept well since I was twenty-one."

A long silence follows while Wesley struggles to find the right words.

"You have spirit. But lack any sense of composure or control. Before you start with the Jian, let me teach you some Chang Quan," offered Sun Tzu.

Placing down the sword, he readies himself in the Cat Stance. Wesley does his best to mimic Sun Tzu.

Moving slowly, in the first few steps Sun Tzu accentuates his breathing. Inhaling as he brings his fist in. Exhaling as he strikes.

THE FAMILY-PART TWO

Neo-Shanxi

Charles Jung

Watching whilst his grandson contemplates his next move, Charles can see the frustration on Alexander's face. Hesitantly his fingers hover over different pieces on the board. Each time he works out his game plan, it has already been pre-empted by his grandfather. Pushing his glasses up the ridge of his nose, Charles knows he has already won.

A cool breeze reminds him that their tea has long since turned cold. From the porch, Li takes a moment out of her painting to check on the two of them. Together they share a feeling of contentment.

The game of chess has been a long and complex one. To his surprise, Charles feels truly tested for the first time in years. His six-year old grandson has provided a better match than any of the players at Salon de Ning.

Finally resigning himself to defeat, Alexander makes the last move of the game.

"You know what that means," said Charles.

"I do the dishes," Alexander admitted, "but before we begin the next match, tell me how you beat me?"

"Age. And that is all that is between us."

Alexander ponders over this for a second.

"Fine. If I win, you take me to Jung Labs."

"And if you lose?"

"I will do the dishes for a week," Alexander said, resetting the board.

Laying down her brush, Li joins the two inside. She wraps her arms around Charles and places a kiss upon his cheek.

"Don't go too hard on him," she whispered into her husband's ear, watching Alexander place the last of his black pieces back in place.

"If only I could," joked Charles.

"Grandfather is very good, Grandma. But he is running out of moves."

She takes a seat to watch the game. "I am sure if you were to ask Grandfather nicely, he would take you to visit the labs."

"A bet is a bet," said Charles.

"Why do you want to go the labs?"

"They seem interesting," explained Alexander, watching his grandfather make the first move.

"Are you interested in science? Is that something you would like to do when you are older?"

Picking up his pawn, Alexander thinks over the question.

"I don't know what I want to be when I'm older. I want to be a good father, like Grandfather."

Charles and Li, touched by their grandchild's sincerity, are deeply saddened by the acute awareness of his parent's absence.

"What would you like to eat tonight?" asked Li, wanting to keep the mood up.

"*Kung Pao.*"

"Would you not like something different tonight?" questioned Charles.

"Nope."

Rolling her eyes, Li turns to Charles. "Something Western tonight?"

"Please. Also, something harder than tea if I'm to face our grandson again."

The sun sets over the colony and the cool day turns into a bitterly cold night.

As soon as dinner arrives, Alexander once again accepts defeat. Helping lay the table while his grandmother brings in her things from the porch, he lays chopsticks for himself and a knife and fork for his grandparents.

The smell of the food brings warmth to the house. Charles pours two glasses of wine and a juice. Walking in to find a prepared table, Li takes her place between the two and toasts their effort.

"Roast dinner, it has been years since we have sat down to a roast," said Li.

"Though it's never quite the same. They can never get the gravy right," said Charles, pouring a gloopy liquid over his plate.

Playfully Li rolls her eyes at Alexander. "Your grandfather is never quite happy with what he has."

Cutting into the largest potato, Charles rolls it in the gravy and places his forkful into his mouth, then the doorbell rings.

Not expecting any guests, he looks over to his wife confused. Li is equally baffled, and just as she is about to answer the door, Charles jumps to his feet insisting that her dinner should not be interrupted.

Opening the door, Charles is lost for words at who he finds on the other side. Waiting on the doorstep is Michael Hastings.

Looking well, he wears the black coat the three of them wore during the terraforming of Delta Nine all those years ago. Charles laughs in disbelief as be holds out his arms to embrace his old friend. Even physical contact is not enough to convince him it's not a dream.

"It's good to see you," said Michael.

"Yes," Charles said, still in shock. "Would you like to come in? We were just in the middle of dinner. Have you eaten?"

"Only if I'm not putting you out."

"Nonsense," dismissed Charles.

Li is taken by surprise as her husband brings Michael in to join them. Ecstatic to see their old colleague, she places down her cutlery, walks over and throws her arms around him, welcoming him into their home. She holds him in place, perplexed at his presence, and they exchange long overdue pleasantries.

Alexander, still sat at the table, observes the stranger with suspicion.

"I cannot believe you're here. It has been so long," said Li.

"Twenty-seven years to be exact," Michael clarified. "You have not aged a day."

"Oh please, you always did know how to flatter a woman. Come, please be seated."

Michael takes a place next to their grandchild. Realising he is being watch, he offers Alexander a gentle nod hello.

"*Hello, my name is Alexander. What is your name?*"

Michael looks around to Charles and Li blankly. He turns to the child and explained, "I'm sorry, my Chinese is not what is used to be. It wasn't very good even then."

"English darling," insisted Li.

Reluctantly he reintroduces himself so that Michael can understand.

"Nice to meet you Alexander, I'm Professor Michael Hastings," he introduced himself, holding out his hand.

Blankly staring at the foreign gesture, Alexander ignores it and pours more Kung Pao into his blow before passing the sizable remains to Michael.

"It is my favourite. I can't eat anymore though. You can finish off the rest for me," he explained with a smile.

"Thank you. I've been wanting to taste some of this famous Neo-Shanxi food."

"Famous food?" remarked Li.

"All those who travel to Shanxi come back with recommendations of where to eat, where to drink and where to hear the best music."

"My mother sings," said Alexander.

"Ah! Well, I'll have to come see her perform sometime."

"Congratulations by the way, Professor," said Charles, changing the subject.

Shrugging off the compliment to hide his awkwardness, Michael tucks into the food. Impressed he gives his approval to Alexander.

"What brings you to Shanxi?"

Li places a hand over her husband's. "Let's not discuss business over dinner."

"Too right, let us enjoy the food," said Michael. "Tell me, how are Alistair and Oscar?"

"My father works at the Labs with Grandfather," said Alexander.

"Oscar," clarified Li.

Figuring that the child is no more than six years old, Michael is confounded at how young Oscar must have been to father Alexander.

"A scientist and a father. When does he find time to sleep?"

"I do question that myself. Three sons, by the way," said Charles.

"Alistair sits in the Assembly with my father. Our youngest is Wesley," said Li.

"And what does Wesley do? A student?"

"No, they closed down the university a long time ago now. Wesley has a job in the metal works. But I have a feeling this will only be temporary," explained Charles.

"I am sorry to hear."

"Don't be. Help yourself to a glass of wine."

"With pleasure," Michael said, pouring himself a modest drink. "Three sons. If I didn't know you better I would say time has made you a better man Charles."

"I'm not so sure about better. Increasingly weary and suspicious would be a fitting summation."

"That's what having three boys will do to you," said his old friend, scooping up another large mouthful.

"Did you ever manage to settle down?" asked Li.

"No," Michael admitted, amused by her question. "I almost had something for a time, but work got in the way. Hence the 'professor'."

"I'm sorry to hear."

"Yeah, me too. Seeing what you have here, you two look happy."

Charles and Li share a smile, and Michael is overcome with a deep sense of loss. Not allowing himself to become emotional he turns to their grandchild who is finishing off his meal.

"You, young sir, have very good taste. This Chinese is the best I have had since I last travelled to China. To be honest, thinking about it, this is much better."

Though pleased by the compliment, Alexander is distracted by the mention of China. "What is Earth like?"

Taking a moment to formulate his answer, Michael decides to be honest with the child.

"If we were on Earth right now, in my flat having dinner, we would look outside the window to see a night sky with a funny green tinge. Earlier in the afternoon the sun would have been blocked out by a sandstorm swept up by the winds and carried across half the globe. Then, if it were to start raining, anyone wanting to nip to the shops would have to wear protective clothing just in case the rain falling is acidic, able to burn your skin. Beautiful flowers and plants like the ones in the gardens outside, struggle to grow in the contaminated soil. Floods destroy communities in what seems like a daily occurrence, while others struggle with thirst as lakes and rivers dry up. Earth is a hard place to live."

"Darling, go and read a book in the living room. We shall join you shortly," Li interrupted.

Dismissing himself from the table, Alexander wanders off looking a little upset.

"Are the CERE yet to construct a TFP?" she asked before Michael could apologise.

"It took a bit of convincing, but they commissioned the project. Though it was built to little avail. No wonder really. Without your genius behind it, the TFP was always doomed to failure."

"Was it under Professor Harrison that the TFP was set up?" asked Charles.

"No, it was under me. Professor Harrison passed away just over a year ago. One-hundred-and-two, the old fart lived longer than anyone expected."

"I'm sorry to hear. I imagine that you two became close after we left," Li offered her condolences.

"We worked with each other, or more like tolerated one another. But despite his ego, I think he really did want the best for humanity. We worked together to terraform planets, expanding the Charted Systems. It was a hybrid of my understanding of your theory and his own ideas. For a long time, it was successful. But upon his death the CERE got reports of two planets undergoing environmental collapse. Muspelheim and Beta Nine."

"And so, the CERE sent you to Neo-Shanxi to drag me back to Earth so I can rescue them from their own mistakes," Charles said callously.

"No," Michael countered, "I'm here on my own accord to ask for your help. To appeal to a man who gave up his entire future to secure one for another people. Charles, without your help thousands of innocent people are going to die."

Charles contends with his conflicting emotions, staring expressionlessly though his old friend.

Michael glances uncomfortably over at Li as she begins to scrape off her plate. Realising there won't be a quick decision made, Michael helps with the dishes. Walking off into the kitchen he accepts Li's gracious offer of the guest room for his stay on Shanxi.

With space to contemplate, Charles fills his glass to the rim and sips the wine. He watches Alexander though the crack in the door. Festering deep inside is an anger at his own complacency. He had protested so little when they closed the university denying Oscar to ever fully realise his aspirations. Silently he sat as Wesley lashed out at a system that alienates the young. What could Alexander ever possibly hope to accomplish on Shanxi?

Oscar Jung

Lingering in the air is the stale alcohol and cooked spices from last night. Staff of the nightclubs brush down the street outside their venue. Small teahouses serve warm beverages to detox all those who have only just recovered from a night of excess. Shops display their wares in the window, most of which are second hand and in need of light repair.

Carrying their own suitcases, Oscar leads his son down towards an address passed onto him by one of his wife's many associates.

Upon arriving, Oscar realises that the block of apartments is a sober house. There is only one doorbell to the whole building. Though the plaque is discreet, this is not the first-time Oscar has visited Xuan living in one.

Apprehensive about leaving Alexander with his mother, he kneels to his son's level.

"I think Mother should come back home while I am away, do you not agree?"

"Yes. I do not want to stay in a place like this again. All the other children are mean and the women swear all the time telling rude jokes," agreed Alexander.

Not ever having considered what it must have been like for Alexander, Oscar is filled with remorse. Looking back at the building he offers another suggestion.

"Maybe you would like to stay with your cousins for a bit. Or keep your Grandmother company while me and your Grandfather are gone? She will get awfully lonely being in that house all alone."

"No, I would like Mother to look after me at home."

With a heavy heart, Oscar complies with his son's wishes.

Before he has an opportunity to ring the doorbell, the front door opens and a gentle young woman answers. She is the sort of person born with an innate sense of goodness.

"Hello. Have you come to visit one of our residents?"

"Xuan Jung. I am her husband, Oscar Jung, and this here is Alexander."

Letting the two inside, the woman insists that they stay in the lobby while she checks whether Xuan would like to receive guests at this time.

Taking a seat on the bench, Oscar inspects the interior. Though plain, the colours of the walls are calming. Down the corridor, a woman is making herself a drink in the kitchen. Uncomfortable with being seen, she closes the door.

Footsteps come down the stairs. The young woman from the banister waves them over. *"Xuan's room is this way."*

Leaving their cases in the lobby, Oscar and Alexander follow her up to the second floor. Turning the corner, they find Xuan waiting at the door to her apartment. Alexander rushes over into his mother's arms. She holds her son close and covers him in kisses.

The woman disappears back down stairs, leaving the family be.

Pleased to see his wife looking healthier than the last time he saw her, Oscar waits patiently to be spoken to.

"Look at you. You look so smart," Xuan said to her son. *"Are you off to anywhere exciting?"*

"We have come to see you," replied Alexander excitedly. *"We want you to come home so that you can look after me."*

Concerned, Xuan shoots a look at Oscar. She whispers something to their son and he walks into the apartment, closing the door to give his parents privacy.

"*What are you doing here? Why did you bring him to me?*"

"*You are his mother.*"

"*What is this really about? Can you not see that I am trying to get clean?*" confronted Xuan tearfully.

"*And I am happy for you. If this was not important I would not be asking this of you.*"

"*Does your grandfather want you to build more trinkets for his secret army?*" she dismissed mockingly.

"*I have to go to Earth,*" said Oscar without breaking eye contact.

Shaken, Xuan is unsure of what to make of the information. Holding her chest, she takes deeps breaths.

"*Why?*"

"*The CERE have requested the aid of Father. Two colonies are experiencing environmental collapse. Without our help thousands of people will die.*"

"*Let them die. Fuck them. Why help them? The CERE take everything from us,*" she argued.

Oscar lets out a weary sigh. "*Because Father has agreed to help save the colonies on the term that Neo-Shanxi is granted independence.*"

"*You fool,*" insulted Xuan. "*They will kill you.*"

Hiding his own fear, Oscar offers his wife a smile farewell.

Making it halfway down the hall, Xuan chases after him. She wraps her arms around him and prevents him from taking another step.

He encases her hands in his, all the things he wishes to tell her are too painful to say. He loves her. Despite all that has happened. The fights. The drinking. The drugs. He still loves her.

"Come back to me."

*

Greeted at the ramp, Oscar's luggage is taken to be loaded onto the Grey Heron. At the top of the launch pad is Michael admiring the view.

Straight ahead, the streets of the Trading District seem to part, allowing for a clear path leading to the Southern Gate of the Political District. Behind that stands the Shanxi Assembly towering over the entire city. Clouds obscure the very top of the Assembly.

Oscar can't help but feel the nerves getting the better of him.

"First time off planet?" asked Michael, not looking for an answer. "Space is like nothing you have seen before. Takes my breath away every time."

"What are other planets like?" Oscar continued the effort made.

"Some vastly different. Others remarkably similar. It is dependent on where in the habitable zone the planet is situated, on the most prevalent minerals and whether there was frozen water beneath the planet's surface. I guess you could argue that Delta Nine is like Muspelheim, in many respects, they are both very red looking rocks. But this planet has a milder temperature."

"I'm looking forward to seeing Earth," admitted Oscar. "Father always used to talk about it when I was young."

Michael senses a sadness in his voice and changes the direction of the conversation. "Whatever you do on Earth, don't order a beef burger or steak. I can't image you've ever had much meat here on Shanxi, it won't do you any good. You'll be in bed for at least a week with an upset stomach."

"Steak?"

"Oh! Let me tell you, humanity has invented the wheel, split atoms, turned light into unlimited clean energy and terraformed distant planets. But my friend, the greatest thing we ever came up with was chargrilled steak. If you ever consider the stomach cramps and the environmental damage of raising livestock a worthwhile sacrifice, only ever ask for it rare," joked Michael.

Charles makes his way up the ramp and greets them both good morning.

"I cannot believe this young man has never had steak."

"Don't eat steak. It will ruin our digestive systems," warned Charles, walking past them. "Come, let's go."

Climbing on board the Grey Heron, Oscar stops to look back at Shanxi one last time before their long journey across the Charted Systems. A hand is placed on his shoulder and his father gestures for him to take a seat.

Faint electrical currents hum through the dual-craft as the engines warm up. Fastening himself securely in the seat next to the window, his father and Michael take the seats opposite. The co-pilot tugs at their belts then yells down towards the cockpit. The second the co-pilot takes his place; the Grey Heron begins to elevate.

Oscar turns pale as they climb altitude. Offering a mint sweet, Michael instructs to suck on it to settle his stomach.

Banking right, the Grey Heron circles around the colony before ascending above the clouds. Directly above the canyon they gaze down at the city which pales into insignificant to the vast surrounding landscape. Even the Shanxi Assembly is nothing compared to the mountains.

Oscar jolts back into his seat as the Grey Heron accelerates through the clouds, up through the stratosphere, until there is nothing more than a thin blue line that separates Shanxi from space.

"Amazing, isn't it?" asked Charles. "My entire life's work. It looks so small from here."

"No, I don't feel like a giant. I feel small," said Oscar.

Though he has seen the images and the research that makes terraforming possible, this is the first time he has ever fully comprehended his father's feats. All those years of measuring margins makes complete sense to him now. Tears begin to form and before he can wipe them away, a single droplet is caught in his eyelashes.

All three of them notice their weight shift. His father and Michael undo their belts and they push themselves from their seats, and appear suspended in space. Unable to contain themselves, the three find a childish pleasure in falling through zero gravity.

Placing Neo-Shanxi between his thumb and index finger, it appears little more than a red marble.

As the distance between them and Shanxi increases, a large vessel appears before them. A ship with large shield like wings protecting a short body. The thrusters concealed in the wings dwarf the Grey Heron. Clumsily pulling himself to the cockpit, Oscar watches in amazement as the vessel increases in stature.

"Well, that puts the ship I came here on to shame," said Michael.

"The Cyclothone. Grandfather's transport ship," uttered Oscar.

Docking into the starboard shield, the airlock is sealed closed while magnets hold the boat in place. Dim red lights pulsate as they wait for the chamber to pressurise.

Loud metallic clicks begin to echo through the hull. The thick metal hatch opens and a bright light shines through blinding all those not prepared.

They are brought through into an enormous hanger with hundreds of other docked Grey Herons. Engineers work hard maintaining and improving the boats. The sheer scale of the operation is something that does not escape either Oscar or Michael's attention. Disorientating enough, the hanger does little to help as more boats are stored above them. Oscar wonders whether it is them who are on the ceiling or if it is the other way around.

"Remember, there is no such thing as up or down in space," reminded Michael.

Drifting out into the Cyclothone, cold cuts through Oscar. Neither his father or Michael seem to be as affected by the dip in temperature. Pulling themselves along to the far end of the hanger, they climb through into a single circular passageway that stretches the full length of the wing.

Cream padding lines the walls. Crew members gracefully float through. Numerous hatches lead off to different sectors. The clinical nature of the ship reminds him of Jung Labs.

"How far are the main quarters?" Michael asked sounding rather worried.

Gently pushing himself off a ridge, Charles drifts off down the column. "This way."

"I'll race you," said Michael to Oscar, slapping him on the back before darting ahead.

Having shown Michael to his quarters, Charles takes his son through to the rear end of the main body. Opening a hatch, he insists Oscar visits this particular room.

Unlike anything else on the ship, the room seems no different from something that would be found on Shanxi. Lavish furnishings with little practicality here in zero gravity. A wall of glass looks out into the void of space. A remnant of the misguided aspirations of his grandfather's original designs. While the rest of the ship has been readjusted, this one single room has been preserved.

"Is this my room?" Oscar asked concerned.

"In a way," Charles began. "This is where you were born."

"This room?"

"In front of the stars," he said with a poetic pleasure. "We were leaving Earth, on our way to Neo-Shanxi when your mother went into labour. There were no midwifes or doctors on board at the time. There was a genuine concern that neither of you would make it. The women that delivered you were simply amazing. Zhang made sure that they never wanted for anything."

With his interest piqued, Oscar takes a moment to let it all in.

"How dangerous is Earth for us?"

"Hopefully not at all. They need our help more than they need us dead."

Wesley Jung

With a pistol in hand, Sun Tzu gives one of his crazed smiles. Even this far back in line Wesley feels as if it is meant for him.

Up front besides him are the other generals of the underground Neo-Shanxi Army. Carefully they inspect their soldiers.

Divided into their respective squads, they stand as a sizable force. Each one of them share a similar story. Each of them now dedicated to fight for the same future.

Squad leaders keep order as they wait for the signal. The competition is simple, to plant their flag at the summit of the largest of the Shanxi mountains. Already the colony seems so far behind them.

Raising the pistol above his head, soldiers chatter and cheer in anticipation. Yong Squad remain silent waiting for the order from Sun Ren as opposed to the gunshot. Squeezing the trigger, the sound crackles through the air.

The other squads race their way towards the mountains, pushing and shoving each other, whilst Yong Squad are left at the starting line.

The dust kicked up by the rest of the army begins to settle.

"No one falls behind. No one races ahead. If you do not reach the top, you are doing everyone else's duties for a month. Move out" called Sun Ren.

She starts them at a slow jog, knowing how much energy they will have to conserve. In sync, they move as a unit. Already the squad can feel the incline.

Wesley stares back at Sun Tzu watching them as they pass the generals. Li Guang calls back, instructing him to play attention.

Across the hills Yong Squad march on, maintaining their pace with regular short rests. They make up for any lost time. The barren landscape leaves the squad exposed to the heat of the sun and with no shade, they must ensure they are well enough protected from the elements.

Day turns to dusk, and dusk into night. Camps litter the hillsides.

Hunched over a portable hop, Wesley and Li warm their dinner for the night. Stirring the broth, Wesley begins to hum an old tune from China.

"*I did not imagine you would be a fan of the old songs*," Li said surprised.

"*Yeah. I used to sing all the time. Not so much recently. I did not think it was the place. Doubt anyone would appreciate it.*"

"*When I was at school I used to be in the choir. Believe it or not.*"

Wesley raises an eyebrow, not sure whether to believe his comrade.

"*Fine, do not believe me. But that is what I always wanted to be when I grew up. Spent years studying music*," he admitted.

"*So, what happened?*"

"*Westerners only want to see young beautiful Chinese girls up on stage, not aspiring young boys. I spent a few years in bars, salons and nightclubs performing on the occasional quiet night to lonely drunks. Angry with being treated with such contempt I eventually stopped working legitimately.*"

Finding out their bowls Wesley begins to share out the broth.

"*Would you ever go back to it?*"

"*Singing? No. There are only so many times people can be rejected. I think that is why I like it here. Everyone is accepted*," said Li contently.

"*I still find it hard to believe. Sing something for us now,*" Wesley teased.

"*I am not giving you a performance.*"

"*Sing for us Private Li. Yong Squad needs a little morale boost,*" Sun Ren commanded from the tent opposite.

The squad encouragingly cheer on their comrade. Though feeling responsible for Li's embarrassment, Wesley can't help but laugh. Quietly their leader waits for him to give into the squads demands.

"*Fine...I will sing an old war song. But first, I want you all to do something for me. Imagine your country, your home, under siege by a brutal enemy willing to resort to the most despicable acts of war. Unable to hold off the invasion, you and your fellow soldiers are forced to take refuge in a warehouse. Low on supplies and nursing injured men, the enemy could strike at any moment. Determined to defend the last free stretch of the city, your commander lies about the strength of the stronghold. Deceiving the enemy. Over the radio, eight hundred names are announced. Eight hundred heroes.*"

The camp falls silent as Li beings to sing the song of eight hundred heroes. Carried by the wind his words reach the nearby squads. Carefully they listen to a feat of bravery in the face of certain defeat.

Wesley cannot help but realise how divorced he is from his mother's native land. A history that has been erased, leaving them all as mere pretenders. With Li still singing, Wesley leaves in search for time away from the camp.

Stargazing, he tries to imagine what the night sky would look like on Earth. A trickle from the forming stream at the foot of the hill reminds him that they are far away from the city. Never in his life has everything seemed so still.

Flickers of light are extinguished one by one as the camps retire for the night.

"*Jung,*" Sun Ren called out.

Sitting up, Wesley welcomes his commanders company. She takes a place next to him and admires the view. Eventually, Wesley lets out a sigh.

"*I feel guilty,*" he confided in her.

Subtlety she studies his features in the moonlight, careful not to be noticed.

"*Because you are the rich kid who got into one too many fights?*" she teased, trying to lighten the mood.

Wesley nods.

"*It does not matter who we once were. I would have thought you had learnt that by now.*"

"*I guess,*" he acknowledged. "*Sun Ren is not your real name, is it?*"

She shakes her head. "*No. It was given to me by Sun Tzu. He told me that even women can be as fearsome and as wise as any man.*"

Unwilling to pry further, Wesley enjoys the silence.

"*Come,*" Sun Ren instructed, "*we have a long day ahead of us tomorrow. I expect us to reach the mining colony by nightfall.*"

*

Feeling the effects of the altitude, Yong Squad press on cautiously. The higher they climb the thinner the air seems. A tight strain throbs across their foreheads. Fatigue begins to set in. Finding out the Diamox tablets from his side pocket, Wesley washes them down with a conservative swig of water.

They know that they must still make their way back down, so each of the squad look out for one another, resting whenever someone begins to fall behind and offering their strength when another cannot go on.

Slumping down against a large rock, Sun Ren in her light-headed daze can scarcely believe her eyes, as she finds herself in the middle of a patch of vegetation growing high up in the mountains. In her hands, Sun Ren carefully caresses a single purple flower.

"Shit, this is so beautiful."

Concerned about their commander, Li offers her a helping hand. *"We should continue Fūrén. Are you alright to carry on?"*

"Yes. I just need a minute."

Wesley notices Sun Ren's broken ankle protruding from the side of her leg, it is a wonder that none of them had noticed until now. Calling over their medic, Li and Wesley keep their commander steady while she is examined. He pulls her trouser leg up revealing a swollen blacked ankle. The sight leaves Li queasy.

"You have badly broken your ankle, Fūrén," the medic informed.

"No," Sun Ren protested, *"I have just twisted it. I will be alright in a minute."*

Wesley holds back is amusement, then catches Li's eye. They both know the severity of the situation. Next in command, Li begins to give the orders.

"We turn back immediately. Once we reach the checkpoint we can radio for assistance."

"Belay that order," Sun Ren perked up. *"If you dare turn this squad around I will have you transferred."*

"Fūrén, you are in no condition to continue."

Grabbing Wesley by the neck, she brings him in close. Able to feel the warmth of her breath, he listens to her request.

"I have not come all this way to fail. We are Yong Squad. We must struggle to become better."

"Jung?" asked Li.

He stares back at their commander, able to sympathise with her resolve. As if carp swimming against the cascading waterfall, they must fight to become dragons. To transcend, they must discard the past. They must elevate themselves above pain.

"It looks like we have a mountain to climb," replied Wesley.

"Well, I am not carrying her."

"You would do well to address me by my title in future Li. And do not dare think that you will be carrying me up this mountain," she cautioned her second in command.

"Well best of luck Fūrén," teased Wesley. *"With that ankle, it would be amazing to see you climb to your feet. Let alone to the summit."*

Quietly the medic agrees with Wesley.

Not completely foolhardy, Sun Ren holds out her hand. Carefully bringing their commander to her feet, Wesley takes the weight as she leans on him for support. They only manage to get a few feet before they both realise the futility of their efforts.

Dropping his backpack, Wesley takes a knee and instructs Sun Ren to grab a hold. Reluctantly she does so. Wesley rises to his feet, to a round of applause from Yong Squad. Li takes the lead ensuring safe footing for the remaining ascent.

"You are insufferably likeable," Sun Ren said so only he could hear.

"I will excuse your comment on the account of the altitude, Fūrén."

Wesley digs his feet into the snow and is helped up the last steep incline. Sweat runs down his brow. His muscles burn. The cold crisp air fills his lungs. Sun Ren feels like a bolder pulling him back down the mountain.

With the last surge of energy, Wesley lunges forward clearing the last few steps. His legs turn to jelly and together they collapse to the ground. Resting his face in the cold, he lays there in disbelief that they made it.

"*Assistance required,*" shouted Sun Ren, rolling off Wesley.

Before anyone can help, Wesley warns off his fellow soldiers and stands on his own volition. The rest of the squad are left dumbfounded at the strength of the young boy from privilege.

He drags himself over to find somewhere to admire the view. Looking out over the clouds that cover the land, Wesley is certain he can see the Shanxi Assembly peeking out in the far distance. How small it all seems from here, as if it were a statue that has been withered down to a grain of sand.

Sun Ren hobbles over and takes a seat next to him. Taking a deep breath, she lets out a sigh of satisfaction. At top the mountain she imagines herself transcended.

Nicholas Jung

Liang Huazhi Square is bustling with people going about their daily business, and an understandably bored Nicholas watches them as he waits for his father's return, while his mother and sister are both off at yet another dressmaker. The concrete bench ordinarily would not offer much comfort, but Nicholas feels as if he has been walking all day.

Behind him the waterway gently trickles. Glancing back for only a second, he notices something sailing downstream. A small paper boat.

Intrigued by his strange discovery, Nicholas fishes the paper boat out before it disappears off into one of the connecting channels. Miraculously dry, he unfolds the boat to find printed in red ink:

'The times test the youth. The youth create the times.'

Though not fully able to understand the implications of the slogan, Nicholas knows that his father would not be pleased to find him with it. Quickly refolding the paper, he places the boat back into the waterway so that it may continue its journey through the veins of Shanxi.

Just as he takes his seat, he is pleasantly surprised to see his father return with two snow cones.

"Thank you, Father," he said with a massive gleeful grin.

"There is nothing more boring than shopping."

"It is the worst."

Leaning over their cones, the two scoop a tiny spoonful of ice into their mouth. They watch the busy square as people rush around.

"Could I become Chairman?" asked Nicholas.

"Not for a long time. It is an important job for a dedicated and hardworking grown up," explained his father.

"Has there ever been a Chairman my age?"

"Great Grandfather is the only Chairman Neo-Shanxi has ever had. Only adults much older than me have been

the Chairman of China. But a very long time ago there were once leaders of China who were your age."

"What were they like?"

"Not good people, largely," began Alistair. *"There was once a Crown Prince, about a year older than you are now, who became the Emperor of Liu Song. When he was younger, he was always getting into trouble. He had a terribly violent temper and this terrible temper did not end when he became Emperor. He would roam his country, killing his people in the most hideous ways. It was a sad day for the Emperor if he had not killed.*

"One day, he woke up his most trusted general and, fascinated by his enormous belly, painted a target on his belly and was about to fire an arrow at him. Just before he let the arrow fly, an adviser stopped the Emperor. He explained to the young ruler that if he shot the arrow at his general's stomach, how could he use it again for target practice. With blunt arrowheads, he embarrassed his most trusted general time and time again," recited his father, trying his best to remember the story.

"What happened to the Emperor?" asked Nicholas, looking rather shocked.

"His most trusted general cut off the Emperor's head while he slept," Alistair finished, now worried that perhaps he had gone too far. *"Sorry. Great Grandfather would tell me and your uncles stories from old China when we were your age. I guess I never thought about how gruesome they actually were."*

"So, I could become Chairman, but I would have to be kind to my people?" questioned Nicholas, pleased his father had shared a moment of his own upbringing with him.

"Yes. Kind and fair."

A shadow is cast over the two sitting on the bench. Looking up Nicholas finds his mother and Jessica re-joining them after their shopping trip.

"*Are you ready?*" asked his mother, with paper bags in hand.

"*Hey, where is my snow cone?*" complained Jessica.

"*How may dresses have you just brought?*" asked their father.

"*Not the point.*"

"*I do not know, Chairman. What do you suppose we do?*" asked their father to Nicholas.

Thinking it over for a second, he studies his sister's disappointed face.

"*We should share our snow cones with Jessica and Mother.*"

"*Share them we shall,*" declared Alistair. "*Come Jessica. We shall share mine together.*"

Before they walk away from the bench, Nicholas turns to check if the paper boat has disappeared. Staring down at nothing but water, his mother nudges him jokingly, insisting on a taste of the snow cone. Nicholas offers her a generous spoonful. Silently he is satisfied with himself, knowing that the boat will reach its destination.

Earth

Charles Jung

"Thank you for joining me," Charles said to Michael who takes the seat opposite.

The whole room is centred around a dried-out tree with white bark. Marble flooring and chandeliers add to the grandeur of the extravagant establishment. Ordinarily it would take months to secure a reservation, let alone a table that overlooks New York City, but the CERE offered to buyout a reservation as a gesture of goodwill. Charles gladly accepted the offer.

Something about the place brings him back forty years to when him and Li would dine at the most exclusive restaurants, rubbing elbows with Earth's elite. Now it seems like such imprudent behaviour in the face of all that has happened.

"Charles, you don't need to be so formal. We are not diplomats. This is dinner between two old friends," said Michael, taking a long hard look at Charles, sensing his unease. "I think Neo-Shanxi has broken you."

"Your right. This is just dinner. Join me in a drink. I think it has had enough time to breathe," said Charles, pouring two glasses of red wine.

"We'd better not get too carried away tonight, a busy day tomorrow. Is Oscar joining us tonight?" he asked.

Charles shakes his head. "I have sent him on a small tour of the city. We will not be staying here on Earth for long, it makes sense for him to see as much of it as possible."

"Ah, so playing the tourist. Anything nice planned?"

"The usual sights mostly. This morning, he was taken over to Ellis Island. Hopefully he realises that all people were once immigrants. Right now, Oscar should be enjoying jazz in the East Village."

"A fan of music?"

"So much of a fan he married a singer," explained Charles.

"Makes sense. How did that work out?" Michael pressed already imagining the story.

"As you might have expected," he said indifferently. "But eventually his work at the Labs grounded him."

Interrupted by the waiter, the two pause their conversation and awkwardly admit they have not yet looked at the menu. Though offered more time by the charming young man, Michael refuses and skims tonight's dishes. Charles sits there clueless and Michael orders for them both.

"My friend here will have the charred chicory cups. I will have the Parma ham with seared scallops and gremolata."

"Good choice sir," the waiter complimented, leaving the table.

"Sorry for ordering for you, but that roast I saw you and Li having on Delta Nine did not look the best and I expect you haven't had much other than Chinese cuisine for decades," said Michael.

"No, thank you. We may have been here all night otherwise," he admitted unoffended.

"Are you prepared for your hearing with the CERE tomorrow? I am happy to give things a once over, to check to see if they are in order. Don't feel as if you have to do it all yourself," pried Michael.

"That will not be necessary. I am as ready as I'll ever be and there is little point in complicating things at this hour," said Charles. "But I would like to ask a favour of you. Instead of accompanying me to the hearing tomorrow, could you escort Oscar to Mianshan?"

"To China?" questioned Michael.

"To the mountains of Shanxi. I would like for him to see it with his own eyes. It would only be for a couple of days while the negations take place. Tickets and travel have already been paid for," he explained. "I need someone I

174

can trust to look after him. Show Oscar the country, the people and be honest."

Michael leans back into his chair, taking a sip of wine he thinks over the proposition. His crystal glass glistens in the light.

All around them waiters serve expensive and specially bred dishes. From the window, the New York City skyline lays under a pea green sky. No stars. The moon only appears as a dim orb from behind a thick fog.

"Will you not need me tomorrow? I have a good relationship with the CERE. Or is that relationship which makes you suspicious?" Michael asked. "I thought it was never about politics."

"Perhaps Neo-Shanxi has broken me," confessed Charles. "For a long time, I refused to accept what it was that my sons had experienced. I had become so passive. But now I fear that either way things are about to change. If I can achieve this without blood being spilt, then I can die content with my life."

The waiter arrives with their starters. Sensing the tension between the two old friends, the young man wastes no time in his service. Impressed that the waiter remembered who ordered which dish, Michael lightens the mood with his gratitude.

Wishing to change the subject, Charles tucks in right away. The sensation of the chicory cups is so overwhelming in contrast to what he has eaten for the past years his eyes begin to water.

"This is so delicious. However, I am jealous of how good yours looks."

"Well you cannot have any unless you want to be bed stricken for the rest of your visit," Michael smugly joked.

"I dare say that it might be worth the risk."

The shared pleasantries quickly come to an end and the two pretend that there is comfortable silence.

Cutting through one of the cups, Charles then gently rests his fork into a sizable mouthful. Guilt washes over him as their reunion has not played itself out as Charles had imagined. Unable to continue with his food, he looks up at Michael with a sincerity that takes both by surprise.

"Sorry for not coming back."

"I told you, family is more important. You did the right thing for yourself and Li," dismissed his old friend.

"Thank you."

"Tell me though," said Michael, waving his fork about. "What did you do wrong to put Alistair off science?"

Laughing to themselves, the two friends do the best they can to put their differences to one side and focus on what really matters. Exchanging stories, their voices becomes lost amongst the laughter and conversation of the restaurant.

In the centre of the marbled hall the white barked tree stands. Though dead, it refuses to decay.

Oscar Jung

Drawing up to the side of the road, Michael switches off the truck's engine. Rusted and old, it was the best vehicle available from the rental outside the Taiyuan airport.

From the city, they have driven for three hours solidly, passing by abandoned towns and a lake created by a nuclear explosion. The Geiger counter installed in the truck has been giving them a general reading of five Sieverts since they left the outskirts of Taiyuan, occasionally it peaked as high as fourteen. Concerned about dust, both have been wearing masks since setting out on their journey to the mountains.

"Come, it isn't far now," Michael reassured his travelling companion.

Getting out of the truck, Oscar gazes at the mountain path ahead of them.

"You are joking?" he called out, feeling exhausted already.

"I'm afraid not, vehicles are forbidden from this point onwards," explained Michael. "You have nothing to complain about, you're not the one who is sixty-odd years old. Get your bag and let's go."

Walking the stone path, there is a sense of ancient majesty about their trek. Met by the occasional gate, Oscar is reminded of the Four Gates of the Political District back home. The mountains seem untouched by the effects of war. Green plants cover the light-coloured earth. Oscar is amazed to see nature behold such beauty.

"Are we still in Shanxi?" he asked naïvely.

"Yeah, we are still in Shanxi. This is Mianshan. We are going to Yunfeng Temple, once home to your grandfather."

The path begins to widen and the two come across a large clearing. Deserted buses litter the area. Straight ahead of them stands a building made of glass. Oscar gawks at the structure bemused by its presence. In the centre of the clearing is a statue of a dragon. Though its vibrant colours have faded, the dragon still stands proudly guarding the temple.

Oscar and Michael press on with the final stretch of their long journey. The slope takes them to a temple hidden in a large cave in the side of the mountain. Having stood the test of time, the red buildings have been adapted to better suit the needs of the people.

Expecting a community of strugglers and intellectuals, Oscar is taken back when he sees that it populated by the kind-hearted and sick.

A middle-aged woman greets them as they wander into the courtyard. The yellow dress hangs from her thin frail frame. She smiles at the two travellers as she holds out a clay bowl filled with water.

"Good evening. You two must be thirsty."

Shocked by her English, Oscar doesn't quite know what to make of the situation. While he tries to calculate the risk of drinking radiated water verses the insult of not accepting the offering, Michael throws caution to the wind and takes a swig. Reluctantly Oscar accepts as she holds out the bowl towards him. Placing his lips around the edge, he is surprised at how fresh the water tastes.

"We do not get many Westerners visiting Mianshan," she said, unintentionally insulting Oscar. "Are you English or American?"

"English," replied Michael, quick to reassure her.

"Ah, good. Are you looking to rest the night?"

"Only if that wouldn't put you out."

Glancing around the commune, Oscar cannot contain his curiosity any longer.

"*Where did the Chairman live?*" he asked in Chinese.

"*You speak our tongue,*" she said surprised, though not sure of which region his accent belongs to. "*You mean Zhang Guozhi?*"

"*I would like to see it if I may.*"

She inspects the two men, sceptical of their reasons for being here. "*You are from Delta Nine?*"

178

"This is Zhang Guozhi's grandchild," interjected Michael. "We have been sent by Dr Charles Jung to visit Yunfeng Temple, so that he can see with his own eyes."

She considers the young man's request and silently complies.

Farther into the cave, they follow her up to a small building that overlooks the whole temple. It is a humble residence in comparison to where his grandfather lives now.

She pushes open the door. The smell of sour milk and excrement hits them. Oscar holds a handkerchief over his mouth as he enters. Rows of cots fill the small building and two young women tend to the needs of the children.

Attempting to step back out, Michael places a firm grip on his shoulder. The middle-aged woman closes the door to keep in the warmth.

In-between the cots, Oscar peers down at the children being cared for. Each child is disfigured. Children with abnormally shaped heads. Patches of hair missing. Underdeveloped limbs. Severely stunted cognitive development.

"Does my grandfather know about these children?"

Staring blankly back at Oscar, Michael waits for him to figure it out from himself.

"Why leave them here?"

"Do you think these children could be cared for on Delta Nine? They are left here because they would be costly dependants. Too much of a drain on the colony's precious resources," rationalised Michael.

Leaning over a cot Michael holds a finger out for the child to grab a hold of. Pleased by the attention, the child's face beams at the stranger.

"On Delta Nine, it would be kinder for them to be peacefully laid to sleep. The strong and able have all been sent to colonises the Charted Systems. Nurseries like this exist all over the country. These are the true children of China."

Neo-Shanxi

Xuan Jung

Carrying an overnight bag, Xuan leads her son up the garden path to her brother-in-law's. Already feeling her stomach turning, she is just as anxious as Alexander.

He hides behind his mother as she rings the doorbell. Despite her best efforts, Alexander refuses to stand by her side sensibly. From the house, she can just about hear the muffled sound of Nicholas and Jessica playing.

The door opens and Weishi welcomes them with a smile. Dressed in her finest black cheongsam with a silver dragon climbing down its front, she is ready for their important dinner with the Chairman.

"*Please come in. Where is Alexander?*" asked Weishi.

Xuan rolls her eyes, hinting at his whereabouts.

Immediately understanding, she crouches down to Alexander's level. "*Well it is a shame that Alexander could not make it this evening. Oh, what a waste. All that food.*"

Appearing next to her mother, Jessica comes to investigate. Waving to her auntie, she is suddenly distracted by her cousin apprehensively peering out from behind his mother.

"*Why is Alexander hiding?*" she whispered into her mother's ear loudly.

"I am not hiding," snapped Alexander.

"Then come and play," said Jessica, grabbing his hand and pulling him into the house. *"Come, I will race you to the garden. We have real flowers growing."*

Weishi steps to one side to allow Xuan to into her home. Leading the way down to the family room, Weishi explains everything that she will need for the evening.

"Thank you for looking after the children at such short notice. We did not know ourselves until this afternoon. But you know their grandfather, keeps everything close to his chest. The first anyone ever hears of anything is when it is happening.

"Dinner is already laid out on the dining table. The food will stay warm for some time, so there is no rush. Sorry that we could not leave you with something home cooked, but I am sure you understand.

"Please do make yourself at home, anything that you need just ask Nicholas. I anticipate that we will be back late so do not feel as if you need to wait up for us. And again, thank you so much."

Only having half listened, Xuan smiles back.

"One of my colleagues told me that you are performing again?"

"Not really. I just get bored," she fumbled over her response.

"I remember the first time I saw you on stage. Salon de Ning has not been graced with a more beautiful voice since. It was as if one of the old greats had been brought back to life. I am glad that you are singing once again."

"I am not so sure my voice is as flawless as it once was," said Xuan embarrassed. *"How are things...at the Assembly?"*

"*Those interested in economics are economists. I will not bore you with the trivial bickering between the SCR and the CERE,*" said Weishi good naturedly, appreciating the effort. "*Please do take a seat, I am just going to finish getting ready.*"

Weishi wanders off down the hall and, when clear, Xuan lets out a deep sigh. Relieved to be alone, she scans the room.

Works of art depict creatures that she has only ever read about and of an evanescent alien world. Ivory and jade figures are proudly displayed in cabinets, each of them a gift to the Chairman in hope they could be better preserved on Neo-Shanxi. A sweet floral freshness fills the house.

Closing her eyes, Xuan dares to imagine what life would be like if this life belonged to her.

"*Xuan?*" said a male voice.

Startled, she turns to find Alistair and Weishi waiting in the hall. Alistair walks over and places a kiss on her cheek goodbye. Still confused by the strange practice, it is something each of the women have had to grow accustom to. Again, Xuan finds herself being told the same thing.

"*Thank you for this evening. I promise that we will be as quick as possible. I am sure Weishi has told you, but there is the guest room down the hall if it gets late. Food is ready. If you have any questions then please ask Nicholas. Jessica will take advantage.*"

"*Ready?*" asked Weishi.

Seeing them off, Xuan watches as they link arms and stroll down the garden path. Sadness outweighs her resentment for the couple.

Once they disappear off into the Imperial Gardens, she gently locks the door. Xuan, feeling the weight of her heavy heart, slumps to the floor, holding back her tears as best she can.

Footsteps slowly approach. Looking up she finds Nicholas standing there, with a cup of tea in.

Alistair Jung

Alistair and Weishi wander around the side of his grandfather's home to a secluded walled garden, following the sound of laughter. Even if they could make out the conversation over the trickling water, neither of them recognise the language spoken.

The Chairman has already brought out the drinks, entertaining his two guests while they wait for his grandchild's arrival. At the table sits a frail old man who looks as if he is permanently stuck in deep thought. The other guest is a beautiful woman wearing a white áo dài. Though they are Eastern, they are not Chinese.

"You have arrived just in time. Please come and meet our guests," welcomed Zhang with open arms. He introduces the old man first. *"This is Nguyễn Hữu Quốc, a good friend and Chairman of the Thuỷ Phủ Assembly."*

Both Alistair and Weishi extend their most hospitable greetings, to only be met with an enthusiastic grunt.

"Anh Quốc does not speak much Chinese," explained his grandfather. *"This is the Mẫu Thoải. First daughter of Anh Quốc, sister to all citizens of Thuỷ Phủ and our translator for this evening."*

"It is lovely to meet you finally. Chairman Zhang has spoken highly of you both," she said.

Weishi takes a seat opposite the woman. *"'The' Mẫu Thoải?"*

"It is merely a title. I am usually not so concerned with political matters. Most of my work is centred around the education and welfare of our least fortunate citizens."

"Considering my husband and his grandfather here at the table, I fear this may be the wrong dinner party for us both," jested Weishi.

"You have yet to see Father get going."

From the house, waiters hired for the night bring out individual bowls for each one of Zhang's guests. Noodles swim in the broth, made from the finest ingredients grown on Thuỷ Phủ. The refreshing aroma of the herbs and the warmth of the spices is unlike anything Alistair has ever experienced before. Wasting no time, he tucks right in.

"This is beautiful," groaned Alistair in pleasure. *"It is so fresh."*

Mẫu Thoải relays the compliments to her father, then translates back.

"Thank you, he says. It is phở, a Vietnamese dish. His father was a chef in Sài Gòn. The only valuable lesson that he was ever taught by him was which flavours complimented one another. Father says he would have cooked himself tonight, but his hands are not the same as they once were."

Inspecting Anh Quốc's hands, they are stiff and ridden with arthritis.

"What happened to them?" asked Alistair, unable to help himself.

"Alistair," exclaimed his wife outraged.

"There is no shame in asking," said Mẫu Thoải. *"Father was involved in the conflicts of South Asia. Once the fighting came to an end, the continent was not better for it. It was then that Father began to help rebuild what was lost. His hands are a lifetime's work of hard honest labour.*

184

As he would argue, a small price to pay. A lesson everyone takes heed of on Thuỷ Phủ. We are fortunate to have such rich soil and it takes hard work to grow and care for our crops. But we build for better."

"*What is Thuỷ Phủ like?*" asked Alistair more appropriately, hoping to win back favour with his wife.

"*A precious gift bestowed upon us by your father,*" Mẫu Thoải translated for Anh Quốc. "*Unlike the barren land of Neo-Shanxi, we have rivers flowing, fields of grass growing, trees spreading their roots. There are no factories processing minerals extracted from the ground, shaping them into utensils or worthless goods. There are no public train lines, instead we travel by bicycle. We live a meeker life. Thriving during the wet season, surviving the dry. Without Thuỷ Phủ, Neo-Shanxi would starve. Yet, without Neo-Shanxi we would perish.*"

"*A true Yang to our Yin,*" added the Chairman.

"*Shanxi is concerned with industrial growth, we with agricultural development. But both have strong political foundations,*" stated Anh Quốc.

"*Two thirds of a Core,*" Weishi quietly remarked, not intending for it to be translated.

"*Exactly,*" said Mẫu Thoải, sharing her father's excitement. "*Father and I are very interested in your thesis, a Tripartite Division of Labour. An interconnected planetary economy based on maximising a planet's natural resources and centralising power to maintain organisation and stability. Your theory has revolutionised our trade with Zeta Nine, Beyul and Maia.*"

"*I cannot believe that you have read my thesis. But how have you manged such a relationship with so few planets?*"

"*In an underhand manner,*" admitted Anh Quốc. "*Zeta Nine, Beyul and Thuỷ Phủ are all bountiful planets. We serve as the Outer-Core. Maia is industrial, rich in minerals and a consistent source of water. As an Inner-Core planet, it alone is not enough to sustain all its dependents. Of course, we have tried to reach out to Epsilon Nine, but the CERE's influence is felt much stronger there."*

"So where does Shanxi lay in all this?" asked Alistair.

"Shanxi, together with Thuỷ Phủ are to become the Core," explained his grandfather. *"That is why we meet tonight."*

"A Core requires political autonomy," noted Weishi.

"At least freedom from the CERE," Mẫu Thoải translated. *"We have a common hindrance. Year after year we strive to atone for our people's past so that we can pave something new. But as we build, the CERE impose colonial policies and ridged trading embargoes. We are governed by a council who do not know what it means to live on other side of the Charted Systems. Governed by those who do not know what it means to be Vietnamese or Chinese."*

"An independence we may soon achieve. My father has gone to Earth to negotiate such demands with the CERE itself," Alistair naïvely argued.

"How likely is it that any meaningful constitutional concession will be made? Forgive me if we do not share your optimism."

"Any other form of declaration would be an open act of insurgency."

"If we were to claim independence irrespective of Dr Jung's negotiations, we would need a sizable armed force, which I am certain neither Shanxi nor Thuỷ Phủ have," Weishi asserted.

Looking back and forth between the two visitors and his grandfather, Alistair then turns to his wife. "*They do. That is why they are here.*"

Weishi places down her chopsticks and spoon. Taking a large gulp of her wine, she attempts to comprehend how she feels about this sudden revelation.

Used to the political games of the Whispering Circle, Alistair finds it hard to believe the sincerity in which the three of them speak. Even the Mẫu Thoải, who came across so benevolent, is part of a conspiracy that may invoke violence against her people. Despite knowing about Sun Tzu and his underground army, there was a part of him that believed his grandfather in wanting to bring structure and discipline to the young.

"*Alistair. Weishi. For the past few years, Neo-Shanxi and Thuỷ Phủ have been formalising an alliance. Acting covertly, we have organised the most distant colonies from Earth according to your Tripartite Division of Labour model. We have secured support from Zeta Nine and Beyul. Maia will soon follow our example, but rest assured that the Chinese on the colony are loyalists,*" clarified Zhang. "*Tonight, we have gathered to ratify our pact. As one, we shall stand against CERE control.*"

Mẫu Thoải presents them with a scroll of parchment made of plant. Laying it out onto the table, both Alistair and Weishi meticulously read through each line of the document. Agreements concerning economic and political rights are explicitly codified. At the bottom is room for five signatures.

"*All that is left to do is to sign,*" his grandfather explained to them, holding out a pen.

"*You want us to sign it?*" asked Weishi.

"You two are the future of Shanxi. Of the Charted Systems. If neither of you sign, none of us will."

Grabbing his hand, Weishi stares deep into his eyes. He squeezes back tight. Not knowing what this will bring, the two of them stand on the edge of uncertainty, waiting for the other to take the first step.

"For Nicholas and Jessica," she whispered.

"Nicholas and Jessica."

Taking the pen from his grandfather, Alistair rests the point of the pen on the parchment. Ensuring his penmanship is perfect, he slowly signs his name. No smudges. No flaws. His name, Alistair Jung, written in black and white. Then, stepping to one side, he watches as his wife signs the pact. Then his grandfather, Mẫu Thoải and finally Anh Quốc.

Ecstatic, Zhang tops up everyone's drinks and marks the occasion with a toast.

"To independence."

Wesley Jung

Roars erupt from their Vietnamese guests as another blow lands between the ribcage of the Shanxi soldier cocksure enough to step into the ring.

On a stack of disused crates, Wesley, Li and Sun Ren sit watching the fight, thankful it is no one from their squad. With her ankle in plaster, she has felt more than useless since coming back from the mountain, even with the support from Li and Wesley. Squinting as their comrade is hit again, Li turns to his commander and both laugh at the misfortune.

Distracted, Wesley meets Sun Tzu's gaze, standing along the balcony with Alistair, his grandfather and the Chairman of Thuỷ Phủ, it feels as if he is being baited by the old man.

The fight ends as blood sprays over the ring. Slow claps commend the soldier's efforts. Others have just lost their bets, doubling their week's chores.

Anh Quốc looks enthralled by the victory, while his brother looks a little queasy. Sun Tzu however does not even seem to recognise the defeat, still fixated on Wesley. With an abrasive clap, Anh Quốc summons another contender into the ring.

A slender young commander steps into the ring. His body taut. A nimble opponent that would be a test of skill and speed. Beckoning someone to fight him, the Thuỷ Phủ soldier is stumped as to why no one is accepting his challenge. Anh Quốc cannot contain his amusement.

Wesley already knows Sun Tzu has been saving this fight for him. From his pocket, he begins to wrap his fists in cloth. Li nudges Sun Ren, drawing her attention to Wesley.

"Do not be fooled. This will be a deceptive fight," she warned.

Following his line of sight, she realises that it is not the Thuỷ Phủ soldier that Wesley is staring at. With the slightest of nods, Sun Tzu gives his instruction.

"Do not embarrass us out there. We are Shanxi's finest."

"Do you really have such little faith in me?" Wesley smirked, jumping down from the crates.

Ensuring the cloth is tight, Wesley throws his top to the floor. Clearing a path to the ring he is met with equal encouragement as mockery.

"So, this is the best Thuỷ Phủ can offer. Some pretty boy and an old man. No wonder the CERE do not fear us. Here I stand before you, a pampered boy from privilege. Come on country boy, I will show you what it means to be Shanxi," taunted Wesley, convinced neither his opponent or Anh Quốc can fully understand him.

Rubbing the ball of his foot into the ring, Wesley controls his breathing. Focussing his strength. Finding balance. The soldier retorts something incomprehensible as he takes his stance.

Hurtling forward, Wesley is only just quick enough to avoid the first strike. The Vietnamese soldier's foot comes crashing to the ground. Using the energy, he throws out his other leg, landing the sole of his foot into Wesley's side.

With no chance to recover, another kick comes flying at him. The speed in which his opponent attacks is nothing like he has ever seen. It is in that moment that Wesley realises how easy Sun Tzu had gone on him.

The Thuỷ Phủ commander throws a wild punch at Wesley in hope to finish the fight quickly. Instinctively reacting to the strike, Wesley finds an opening and scores his first hit. Finding space once again Wesley hopes to dictate the flow of the fight.

Any control he gained, is lost in the next onslaught. Struggling to keep up, more punches being to slip though. Blood trickles from his nose after a what felt like a slight knock.

Sniggering to himself, Wesley begins to question his opponent. For all his skill, how many times has he taken a beating. Dropping his guard, Wesley puts all his weight behind his fist. A loud crack silences the whole room.

A throbbing pain burns in his side. Despite it feeling like his ribs are broken, he knows the sound came from the young Vietnamese soldier. Brought to his knees, blood dribbles onto the ring. He attempts to find his feet, for only Wesley to bring down another punch. His body hits the floor with a thud.

"*Jung, enough,*" Sun Ren's muffled voice cried.

Scanning the room, fellow soldiers chant and cheer. Sun Ren stands with a glint of fear in her eyes. Ignoring the hysteria of his commander, Wesley turn to the balcony.

Alistair has the same look across his face, unable to recognise his own brother. His grandfather and Anh Quốc quietly converse as they head towards the exit. No one who matters stays to relish in his victory.

Above, Sun Tzu stares back with his crazed smile.

*

His side is already coming up in a nasty purple bruise. Their medic had to put stitches where his lip split. A lingering metallic taste won't leave his mouth.

Ensuring his squad are fast asleep, Wesley sneaks out of their quarters and heads through the underground corridors to find Sun Tzu. For months of mentoring, it was not skill that won him tonight's match. Concentration and focus only held him back, leaving him uncertain in the lesson he was supposed to be learning.

As with most nights the old man is in his chamber, but something is different. Instead of practicing, he waits for Wesley at the far end of the room. Holding out his palm, Sun Tzu instructs the young soldier to come no farther. In the middle of the room is his sword, dividing the two men.

"If I collect the Jian before you, I will plunge it into your heart," threatened Sun Tzu. *"If you collect it before me, I will beat you like you beat that Thuỷ Phủ commander."*

"You will not kill me," Wesley scoffed. *"I am tired of your games. They make no sense."*

Sun Tzu hangs his head disappointedly. *"You are strong. In both body and spirit. Arrogant too. A quality that will get you killed on the battlefield. More importantly, it will endanger the lives of your squad and those who you wish to protect. Why should I spare such a liability?"*

Without thought Wesley tuts, dismissing the musings of the old man. How could his mentor be so conceited to ignore all that he had achieved since being conscripted? Proving himself time and time again, Wesley decides this has nothing to do with what he does, instead who he is. Giving up on winning his mentor's respect, Wesley turns to head back to bed.

"Do you not consider me serious boy?"

"No."

Sun Tzu makes a run for the sword. Purely reactionary, Wesley dives across the room, landing hard and manages to place his fingertips on the blade. Quickly he draws the sword closer, gripping the hilt tight. True to his word, Sun Tzu toe punts Wesley in the face and the stitches come undone.

Swinging wildly, the tip of the blade manages to cut into the flesh of the old man. Impressed, Sun Tzu does not wait for his apprentice to find his feet. A single kick knocks him back down.

Weaving in and out of the cautionary swipes, Sun Tzu does not waste time in finding the first opening. Twisting Wesley's wrist, he places enough pressure to cause his hand to open, dropping the sword. Sweeping his feet away, Sun Tzu retrieves the weapon.

Wesley feels a sharp pain pinning him place. Sticking into his chest is the cold metal. Though not fatal, it is deep enough for Wesley to worry about the damage done. Slowly Sun Tzu twists the blade.

"*Fuck,*" roared Wesley. "*Just tell me. No more games.*"

"*You are about to face real monsters. Animals who will show no pity. When it begins, there will be no heroes. Just those who live and those who die,*" he explained.

Pulling the sword from his chest, Sun Tzu finds a cloth to wipe it clean. Wesley lays there, heart pounding, beads of sweat running down his skin. Blood covers the dragon crawling up his neck.

Oscar Jung

The old family home is a comforting sight. All the downstairs lights are on, which means only one thing. Oscar imagines his mother in the kitchen helped by Wesley and Weishi, while Alistair hopelessly struggles with the menial task of cutting the vegetables. His grandfather telling Alexander and his cousins myths from the old country. He wonders where his wife is tonight.

Utterly exhausted from their voyage home, neither Oscar or Charles can find it within themselves to be pleased with their return. Both are troubled by their failure and unsettled about what will happen next.

Just as his father is about to ring the doorbell, Oscar stops him and for a second, he struggles to find the right words. "Thank you. For bringing me along. Even if, well, you know."

Charles nods. "You don't ever have to say thank you. Just do me a favour, don't tell your brothers about China. It is something you have to see with your own eyes."

Oscar agrees.

The bell is rung and they can hear the excitement coming from the house. Small but loud footsteps come racing to answer. Barely opening the front door, Alexander throws himself into his father's arms. Holding him tight, Oscar looks over his son's shoulder to find Xuan awkwardly standing beside his mother.

"You were gone for so long," said Alexander tearfully.

"I am here now."

Taking Alexander by the hand, he leads them over to Xuan. Nervously she taps her heel, shaking her whole body. With no need for words, he embraces his wife. She glances over at his parents to see them both smiling.

"It is good to have you both back safely," said Li, placing a kiss on Charles' lips.

"Are they back?" Alistair's voice called out from somewhere in the house.

"Tend to the noodles," instructed Zhang, emerging from the kitchen. *"Wesley, do you mind supervising the dinner. I fear it may take more than Weishi to avert your brother from causing a disaster."*

"Yes Grandfather," Wesley obliged.

Jumping up from the floor where he was playing with Nicholas and Jessica, he quickly welcomes his father and brother home. He places a firm grip on Oscar's shoulder.

"You look well brother. It is good to have you back."

"You were prettier the last time I saw you," joked Oscar, inspecting the cut on his lip.

With a wink, Wesley laughs. He turns to his nephew and niece. *"Come on you two. Dinner is almost ready and the table is not set."*

Xuan leans down to Alexander. *"Come, we should help out. Your father needs some time to rest, we will have plenty of time to hear about their trip to Earth later."*

Understanding his son's disappointment, Oscar quietly mouths that he will join them shortly. Even with the reassurance, Alexander is reluctant to be separated so soon.

With the children having been taken into the dining room, Zhang is quick to get his pleasantries out of the way.

"I expect you feel like you have not had a proper night's rest since leaving Shanxi. I know you had time on the Cyclothone, but if you ask me, sleeping in zero gravity is never quite the same. Isn't space a miraculous sight though."

"Like nothing I have ever seen before," answered Oscar, finding it hard to match his grandfather's enthusiasm.

"Yes, well. I expect you are both tired. It will be nice for you to unwind with the family tonight," he said. "Li, if you do not mind, may I steal Charles for a couple of minutes?"

"Of course," she said. "Son, you could probably do with a drink anyway."

Oscar is left with his mother while his grandfather ushers his father into a private room of the house. Slumping on the sofa, Li fixes them a drink. Pleased that his mother is the only one around, he feels as if he can finally relax. She knows what he has seen and there does not need to be any pretence between them.

"Young Alexander has missed you dearly. Xuan has done a remarkable job," said Li, handing over the drink.

"I expect she has not done it alone."

"There is no shame in asking for help Oscar," she explained. "Whatever happened on Earth, put it behind you. You are back with your family. This is where things matter."

Hanging his head, Oscar does his best to hold back his emotions, but cannot. "We failed. We failed everyone. Muspelheim, I tried Mother. I tried."

Silently she consoles her son. Li listens, not pressing for needless details, unlike the interrogation she envisions her husband is undergoing from her father.

"Whatever Harrison did, screwed the planet. By the time me and Michael reset the TFP, it was too late. Bodies lay scorched in their homes. The smell...I can still smell it," said Oscar, taking a swing of his drink. "It was the same for Father on Beta Nine. We were too late. The CERE refused to honour their agreement to grant constitutional change to Shanxi. They said we did not meet the conditions of the agreement. They acted so callously. No regard for all the colonists lost."

Placing her hand over his, Li does not disguise her honesty. "Your father was foolish to think the CERE would honour any promise. But you did the right thing. You tried to save those people. The good that you did, even if it met an unfortunate end, separates us from them."

"Thank you, Mother," muttered Oscar, squeezing back.

"We should join everyone in the dining room. Wouldn't want the food to go cold."

Li kisses her son on the forehead and stands waiting for him.

The pop of a cork startles Oscar as he enters the dining room. His family gathered around the table cheer, delighted to have him home. A banner made by the children has been hung along the wall and a vast spread

196

has been laid out. Wesley begins to pour out glasses of champagne, one of the last bottles in their parent's reserve. Taking a seat between Xuan and Alexander, Oscar is humbled by the fuss his family has made.

"*It is good to have you home,*" Weishi said, serving up the last of the dinner.

Finally, Alistair places a bowl of noodles in the centre, impressed with the one dish he was allowed any control over.

"*The best noodles on the whole of Shanxi. Forget all this other fancy food,*" he said boastfully.

"*They look a little soggy,*" Wesley jested to the children's amusement.

"*Soggy noodles are good noodles. No?*"

"*Well, I am sure we shall all stomach them for your sake,*" Weishi joined in.

Jessica whispers something into her uncle's ear and together they quietly conspirer from across the table. With a slight of hand, Wesley steals a jiaozi for his niece. Inauspiciously Jessica attempts to eat it without her father noticing. Catching them in the act, Alistair is unsure of who to scold. Wide eyed, Wesley stares at his brother trying to break his serious glare.

Joining them at the table, Zhang and Charles take their places. Li checks in on her husband, gently he reassures her. Standing with his glass in hand, their grandfather waits patiently for everyone's attention. Wesley rolls his eyes at Oscar jokingly before holding out his glass.

"*Thousands of families sit down to dine tonight. Not just here on Shanxi, but amongst the stars. We are fortunate to have one another. Family is what makes us strong. Family is what makes us belong. For all those thousands of families together tonight, there is none like this one. It is*

197

our family that gives me hope and fills me with the greatest sense of pride," toasted Zhang.

"Aww," Wesley sarcastically interrupted.

Taking it in his stride, Zhang permits everyone to begin the feast, much to Jessica and Alexander's relief.

The food is passed around. Drinks refilled. No one is left out from conversation. Momentarily Oscar's spirits are uplifted, forgetting about all that he had witnessed.

After dinner, the Chairman heads outside for fresh air, while everyone else heads into the living room to play games. Sitting amongst his children, Alistair enjoys the informality of the evening. Xuan does her best to follow Alexander's instructions to win the game. Wesley shares his story of climbing the Neo-Shanxi mountains with their mother.

His brother's feat leaves Oscar feeling sombre, recollecting his own expedition into the mountains of China. Sneaking away, he joins his grandfather out on the porch.

"How did you find Earth?" asked Zhang, wistfully gazing up at the stars.

Hesitantly, Oscar answers. *"You lied to us."*

"How so?"

"I have seen China. It is a desperately sad place."

"But a country with dignity…" the Chairman began, being cut off quickly.

"No. No it is not," refuted Oscar with a crackle in his voice. *"The land is barren, saturated in levels of radiation too dangerous for humans to live off. Whole regions of the countryside abandoned. The people are starving. Babies are born deformed and disowned by their parents. Cities are a cesspit, swelling with a population of the desperate*

and the depraved. You have fooled us all in thinking that you are some saviour and that we are at all Chinese."

"*Then what are you?*" the Chairman pressed tactfully.

"*I am a bastardisation of whatever remnants you managed to salvage from a dead culture,*" he admitted. "*I am Shanxi.*"

Zhang stands from his seat and wanders over to the banister.

"*And thankful we must be. Your father and I did not bring you here to be Chinese. We brought you here to be better. If Shanxi is what you must be, then be it.*"

"*Why did you makes us believe in China?*"

"*Heritage,*" he explained. "*All great civilisations do it. Fabricate myths about some fantastical paradise or past. If no one believed, then why should we fight for better? I have given all to provide better for our people. For my family.*"

"*And what does that better look like?*" Oscar questioned.

"*Tomorrow, the whole of the Charted Systems will see. A truly independent Neo-Shanxi. Free of the CERE. A new start for the people. You and your brothers will be instrumental in that future. It is my gift to you,*" he said with a sense of accomplishment.

"*I never asked for that responsibility.*"

"*Yet it is your duty,*" concluded his grandfather, placing his hand on Oscar's back and giving him a look of unwavering conviction. "*Come inside, I can feel a storm brewing.*"

Alone, Oscar watches as clouds gather along the horizon. Contemplating his grandfather's words, anger washes over him for allowing Zhang to sidestep taking any responsibility.

199

Startled by the door sliding open, Oscar turns to find Xuan coming to join him. Taking her place besides him, she looks out into the distance.

Apprehensively, he takes her hand. "*I am sorry. I never realised how lucky I was.*"

Wesley Jung

Wesley tightens the straps arounds his arm. The armour is well fitted and surprisingly it is incredibly light. At first the exoskeleton constricted movement, but as the microfibers adjust, they begin to mimic the muscles of the soldier. Though certain they are not going to meet any real resistance, it is a concern of how well the suit will protect them when they do.

Li brings over Wesley's helmet and takes a seat next to him. Wesley studies his reflection in the orange visor.

Sun Ren limps into the room and Yong Squad stand to attention, waiting for further instruction. With a stencil and spray can in hand she addresses her soldiers.

"*The Political District is under lock down. An emergency alarm has been sounded to keep citizens in their home. Soldiers are gathering the members of the Shanxi Assembly as we speak. Yong Squad have been instructed to escort the Chairman and prominent members of SCR from the Imperial Gardens to the Assembly. Once the vote for independence has been cast, we are to aid in rounding up any opposition.*

"*On the way through the training hall, each of you will be issued a rifle and a single clip. This is for defensive purposes only and only to be used if all other possible options have been exhausted. Understood?*"

"*Yes, Fūrén.*"

Placing his helmet on, the word '*calibrating*' flashes up in the corner. Wesley sniggers amused. With their identities concealed, their commander goes around spraying '*brave*' onto each of their chests.

One last time she has them recite the squads five rules.

"*You let one down, you let all down...Individuals die, units survive...Broken windows lead to broken limbs...Sun Tzu is absolute...Chinese we are, Chinese we will stay.*"

"*Move out.*"

Through the deserted streets of the Political District the Yong Squad march their personnel towards Liang Huazhi Square. At no point in his recent memory can Wesley remember the colony being so silent. Coincidently he finds himself escorting Alistair and Weishi. As instructed he does not communicate with his brother.

Other than Sun Ren with her limp, Sun Tzu is the only soldier that can be identified. Helmetless, he takes the lead with the Chairman.

The Shanxi Assembly has already been seized. Soldiers guard the entrance. In the centre, the Shanxi Dragon welcomes them in.

Tripping on her way up the steps, Wesley rushes to steady Sun Ren. She thanks him and together they take each step slowly. Weishi offers her help to the young commander, but is politely refused. They climb into the elevator with his brother, while Zhang and Sun Tzu take the other one.

Riding the elevator all the way up to the Whispering Circle, nerves begin to set in. Several of the soldiers' mutter something incomprehensible to themselves. Li anxiously taps his foot. Wesley feels his stomach cramp up.

Sensing the nerves of the soldiers, Alistair tries to put their minds at ease. "*You are all part of something great. In years to come, they will mark today as a triumph for the people of Shanxi. No, not just for Shanxi, but for all the colonies of the Charted Systems.*"

"*Thank you, Minister Jung,*" said Sun Ren.

The doors slide open, Sun Tzu and the others are already waiting for them. He explains to the Chairman that the Assembly has already gathered in the hall. The muffled outrage of the ministers fill the circle. The situation is already tense.

Marching into the hall, the sudden presence of the Chairman accompanied by soldiers sends the Assembly into chaos. Ignoring the cries and abuse, he takes his place at the head of the Assembly. Forcefully he demands order. When he does not get it, Sun Tzu fires a few warning shots into the ceiling.

"*What is the meaning of this Chairman Zhang?*" asked Du Jianguo of the SC.

"*I am sorry my friend, I wish this could have happened any other way,*" Zhang offered a personal response despite his better judgment.

"This is a coup. You will be executed for this," threatened Israel Epstein of the CERE.

Before he can continue with the outburst, Sun Tzu drags him out of his seat and hits him with the butt of his rifle. Falling to the ground, the shock of the violence silences the Assembly. Even his own soldiers are startled.

Taking control of the hall once again, the Chairman address his ministers.

"*I have summoned you here today to restore sovereignty to the people of Shanxi and to reinstate a constitution which was unlawfully and undemocratically renounced by the CERE. Too long have we been complicit to a tyrannical foreign power that denies our people liberty and opportunity. Our colony's resources are exploited for the monetary gain of Earth based corporations. They drain our planet, refuse to reinvest in the colony and cause environmental damage that if gone unchallenged will lead to irreversible damage.*

"*I put it to the Assembly, that all unelected bodies, not chosen by the people of Neo-Shanxi, are to be deemed illegal. How does the Assembly vote? In favour?*"

Erupting once again, the minster's objections are snuffed out by the reminder that they are at gunpoint. The CERE refuse to engage in the process. Joining their protest is Du Jianguo and the Shanxi Conservatives' top party members, Li He and Yao Hongwen.

"*Motion is passed,*" declared Zhang, irrespective of the result. "*Next proposal. Any political or business enterprise that currently holds interests that conflict with the sovereignty of the Neo-Shanxi Assembly and its people, are to be detained and prosecuted as conspirators. Those members of the Assembly who fail to denounce their affiliation with the CERE, will be detained and prosecuted as collaborators. Those who oppose, please rise.*"

Israel stands to his feet, looking down on Sun Tzu with a sense of superiority. Even Sun Tzu's crazed smile does not intimidate him.

Du joins the majority of his party in defiance. Impressed at the bravery of her peers, Li He begins to applaud them. The commotion only makes the situation worst.

A member of the CERE looks to make their escape. Hoping to slip out unnoticed, they try to sneek past Li and Wesley guarding the exit. With everyone distracted by the upheaval, they make a run for it. The door slams shut.

"Do not let them escape," Sun Ren ordered.

Bursting into the Whispering Circle, the two soldiers chase down the run-away politician. Already in the elevator, Wesley knows how easily they could lose them in a building this large. Looking down the sight of his rifle, he aims for the shoulder.

"No," screamed Li.

Wesley loses focus, but already he has begun to squeeze the trigger. A single shot is fired. The elevator doors close shut before either of them can see what has happened. Screams come from inside the hall.

Calling the elevator back up, both Wesley and Li hold their breath. The doors slide open, blood paints the back wall. Laying on the floor is the CERE politician with a hole through their neck.

"Hide the body," instructed Sun Ren as she approaches. *"We have to use these to get the others down to the police station. Jung, when it is done, stay here and look after the Chairman. There were not supposed to be any casualties."*

"Sorry, Fūrén."

"It is not me who you need to be sorry to."

Seeing the last of the collaborators out of the hall, Wesley sits in the empty benches. The realisation of what he had done is yet to sink in. Behind the armour, he feels detached from his own actions. The guilt he feels is from not feeling guilt.

Du is the last to be marched out, attempting one last time to reason with his old rival and friend.

"You have made a grave mistake Zhang."

"My mistake was thinking that we could work with the CERE. One that even now you are committed to. It is not too late. Your council over the years has been invaluable.

Imagine what we could achieve now that we are free," the Chairman argued.

"Freedom that was won at the barrel of a gun. A freedom that has already been paid for in blood," said Du, looking at Wesley.

"Yes, well that was unfortunate. But scarifies may be necessary if we are to achieve a better tomorrow."

"Sacrifices?" Du sneered. *"Does that include your grandchildren?"*

Wesley realises that the former minister has figured out his identity.

"My grandchildren know the struggle that lay ahead of them. They have made their choice, as much as you have made yours," explained Zhang.

"When does that sacrifice become too high?"

"Yīn yè fèi shí," dismissed the Chairman.

"Bú shàn shǐ zhě bù shàn zhōng," Du retorted.

"Farewell my friend," finished Zhang with a heavy heart.

Two soldiers escort Du out of the hall. Even though the Shanxi Chinese Representatives occupy the assembly, it seems quiet. Weishi is busy organising her new cabinet, ready to restructure the whole of Shanxi economics. Others find the time to gather their thoughts on the morning's event. It has all happened so swiftly.

From the floor, Alistair gestures for Wesley to come and join him. Surprised that he even figured out his identity, Wesley concludes he must be giving it away somehow. Climbing over the benches, he joins his brother in the Whispering Circle, looking out at the colony.

It is a clear day and the view stretches out for miles. Below them the beauty of the city seems more vibrant than usual. Rooftops glisten with the residue of last night's storm.

"*I knew it was you,*" he said with a smarmily grin across his face. Alistair must not have realised it was Wesley who shot the CERE member. "*I think it is your height.*"

"*So, this is it?*" asked Wesley.

"*Yes. This is it. Today, Shanxi is waking up to a new dawn.*"

"*Funny, it feels no different from yesterday,*" he joked.

Alistair places a hand on his brother's shoulder. "*Wait until you breathe in that morning air.*"

Worms

Gas fills the corridors of the police station. The Neo-Shanxi soldiers lay collapsed on the floor. Like ghosts, soldiers dressed in black and blue scout the station. Masks obscure their breathing. Large blackened lenses make them resemble bugs more than anything human.

Finding their way to the cells, another gas grenade is thrown down the steps. Panic spreads. Gasping for air, one by one the detained politicians fall asleep. Du waits in his cell. Holding his breath.

"Waltzing Matilda, waltzing Matilda. You'll come a-waltzing Matilda, with me," sang an Australian voice.

A gasmask is thrown through the bars. Scrabbling to put it over his head, Du looks up at the singing soldier. The insignia on his armband is ambiguous, as if it were a mound of worms. The soldier kneels to his level.

"Thank you for your help, it is much appreciated," said Worms. "Don't worry about these bars. They are only temporary. Patience, Chairman Du. Patience."

Worms pulls off the mask and waits for him to inhale the gas. Preparing for the imminent nightmares, Du rests himself against the bars and drifts off to sleep.

REVOLT ON MAIA

Maia

Wesley Jung

The great gas giant of Thule eclipses the solar system's star. A marble of different shades of beige flow around the planet. Occasionally a dim flash illuminates the clouds. Storms more ancient than humanity rage on. Its two moons are but specks compared to such a giant. Maia has seen its last rays of light for forty-eight long, dark hours. As it orbits around Thule, temperatures will dip to below freezing. Snow has already begun to fall.

Not a single soldier on board the Grey Heron has been off planet. None of them have seen anything but the red earth of Neo-Shanxi. Below them is a brown rocky surface. Large bodies of water form what could only be described as seas. The soil is rich in minerals, but vegetation struggles to survive the sudden freeze of each cycle. For the soldiers of Yong Squad, Maia is a truly alien world.

In the shadow of Thule, they begin their decent into Maia's atmosphere. The vessel begins to shake violently. The hull creeks and moans. Wesley holds his restraints tightly. Looking at his fellow soldiers, each of them appear just as queasy.

"If you throw up over yourself, you will have to go into battle wearing it. We do not have any spares. My best advice is to just swallow," said Sun Tzu, sensing the feeling of the boat.

Knowing him, he means every word of it. Wesley leans his head back and closes his eyes. Just as things settle, they hit another pocket of turbulence. The soldier next to him begins to gag and Wesley prays he does not vomit his way.

"Two minutes to touch down," called the pilot.

Unbuckling himself, Sun Tzu wraps his hand around the grips, steadying his balance. Standing in the aisle, he addresses the squad.

"Listen up. This is the last moment of peace that you will have until this is all over, so let us make sure we are clear on the situation. Our LZ is on the outskirts of the Lotus Gardens, a Chinese residential district. There we will rendezvous with the Chinese civilian resistance. While Shanxi and Thuỷ Phủ forces secure the area, Yong Squad are to immediately assist the locals in pushing the conflict back into the central industrial district of the Foundry.

"We are the vanguard. Success of this mission is dependent on us. We will be met with heavy resistance from Western colonists armed with military grade firearms. How they obtained them is unknown. Despite this, our primary objective is to stabilise the colony, so casualties are to be kept to a minimum. Any injured civilians are to be brought back for medical attention. Understood?"

"Sir," confirmed the squad.

Thrusters being to slow their decent and the landing gear is prepared. Wesley lets out a sigh as they touch down. The nerves of the squad do not settle.

With Sun Ren's ankle still recovering, she has been given control of Shanxi's security. Sun Tzu in her stead has taken command of the Yong Squad. Many right now would be comforted by the presence of their commander leading them into battle.

The engines quieten to a purr and are replaced by the crackle of gunfire. Out of the window, beyond the residential district, clouds of smoke rise from the canal. The occasional explosion sends debris flying.

"*Doors opening in ten, nine...*" warned the pilot.

"*Ready yourselves,*" Sun Tzu ordered.

Wesley secures his helmet and fetches his rifle from overhead. The visor displays his vitals, satellite imagery, highlights fellow soldier's status, among many other things. Feeling overloaded by the amount of information cluttering his vision, Wesley only has the essentials active.

The hatch slides open and an icy rush of wind blows in. Before any of them can shudder, the exoskeleton regulates their temperature.

"*Move out.*"

Jumping out from the boat, they look around the field to find the rest of the Shanxi Army arriving. The dark sky is filled with the blinking of landing lights.

Already Sun Tzu is marching towards the resistance camp, wasting no time. Together, Wesley and Li take a moment for it all to sink in. Irritated, their leader calls for them to keep in line.

There are aspects of Lotus Gardens that remind Wesley of home. The architecture and colours are distantly Chinese. Streets are close and narrow, which occasionally open to large quads. A labyrinth like layout is the only reason the Chinese colonists have manged to hold out so long.

The injured and dispossessed litter the streets. The sudden arrival of armed soldiers is a welcome sight. Most of the citizens have fended off the attack with nothing more than rocks, glass bottles, kitchen utensils and the few guns they managed to scavenge. A struggle that would have not been able to hold out for much longer.

The resistance camp is barricaded by furniture dragged out from the nearby houses. A thick layer of dirt covers everything and everyone. All the men and women look weary. Deprived of sleep, they hope to doze off between the breaks in fighting.

The Yong Squad are met by a young man whose face is covered in ash. He leads them over to a small table where several colonists are hopelessly assessing the situation.

"Who is in charge?" Sun Tzu yelled over the noise.

"No one," admitted the young man. *"It is just those able to fight. Who is asking?"*

"Sun Tzu, General of the Neo-Shanxi Army," he said. Even though his face is concealed under the helmet, Wesley can sense the smirk across his face. *"Is this your base of operations?"*

"As close as you are going to get," replied one of the women around the table.

A map of the city is laid out on the table. It has clearly been drawn from memory as the satellite imagery highlights so many inconsistences.

The colony is divided into three zones, sectioned by canals. Their current position is in the northern region of the colony and the second largest. The largest is Southside, the Western residential district. In the middle is the Foundry, an unregulated industrial powerhouse which dwarfs the productivity of the Industrial District back on Shanxi.

Crosses and whole regions have been blacked out, marking the loss of the colony and failed assaults. Carefully Sun Tzu studies the map, a gesture of courtesy as opposed to learning anything meaningful.

"We have as many people as we can spare along the canal," said the woman, pointing at the line that separates

the Lotus Gardens from the Foundry. *"But we have lost a lot of people holding that line. There are people trapped in the central district, but we have no way of getting to them."*

"When did you last have contact?" asked Li.

"A few days ago," said a young man. *"It sounded like they were being hunted. Then nothing."*

Hearing that sends a shiver down Wesley's spine. He glances around to see if the others are as equally spooked, instantly reminded that none of them can see each other's faces.

Against the murky backdrop, each of the Shanxi soldiers stand out in their pristine mossy green armour. They all stand out as clear targets.

"There must be a weak point in their line," Li checked with Sun Tzu.

"Here is as good as anywhere else," another woman said.

Sun Tzu marches off alone to the barricade. Climbing as high as he can, he scouts the nearest bridge. Beyond the ruins of the Lotus Gardens, Western colonists have taken cover behind a similarly built blockade. A few have taken shelter in the warehouses on either side of the street. Jumping back down, Sun Tzu rounds up his squad.

"Tell all stations to hold their position until back up arrives," Sun Tzu instructed the colonists.

Stray bullets fly as Yong Squad make their way through to the front line. It becomes quickly apparent that they are up against an enemy with no real training. The kick back from each round makes for a terrible shot. Regardless, Sun Tzu is not willing to take any risks and darts from cover to cover. Wesley follows close behind Li.

Resting his back against the wall of the canal, the two of them take a second to catch their breath.

"*Li and Jung, you are with me,*" ordered their general over the coms.

Stepping out onto the bridge, the three of them are completely exposed. Wesley's heart beats so fast it feels like it might burst. Heading straight down the middle, the rest of the squad pull up the rear, laying down covering fire.

Targets are identified on screen, tracking their movement. Aiming for the shoulder, Wesley squeezes the trigger. Falling to the ground, the first of the Westerners is neutralised. Screams pierce through the volleys of gunfire.

Along the canal the fight intensifies as the Chinese colonists are joined by Shanxi and Thuỷ Phủ troops. Flickers of light burst as other squads advance towards the Foundry.

The Yong Squad are supported from behind as Shanxi soldiers secure a defensive line. Seeing the strength of the force, most of the Western colonists fall back, only the brave and foolish stay to fight.

Clearing the bridge, Sun Tzu orders for the injured Westerners to be rounded up and ferried back to the resistance camp to receive medical attention. Though the Westerners protest, they are too incapacitated to put up any real struggle. Their weapons are confiscated and dismantled. The sophistication of the rifle surpasses their own *Dragon Crescent*. For Sun Tzu, it seems unlikely that there would be the expertise on Maia to develop such technology.

Wesley finds the man he shot in the shoulder propped up against the barricade. A trickle of blood runs down his thick jacket. Spluttering something unintelligible, Wesley offers his hand out to the Westerner. Instantly it is slapped away. Kneeling to the man's level, he hopes to reason with him.

"Do you speak English?"

"Bits," replied the man bemused.

"There is a medical centre being set up in Lotus Gardens. We can get your shoulder seen to."

"I do not need help, Chinese dog," spat the man.

"We are not here to fight. We want peace on this colony as much as you do," explained Wesley.

"Lies," shouted the man desperately, shocking Wesley. "Lies which have already been told."

Despite Wesley's best intentions the man continues to protest. Soldiers come and carry him away, he thrashes about with all his weight.

The cease fire was a short but welcome break for all. The reinforcements have given much-needed relief to the exhausted civilians. Already in the camp, abandoned buildings are being converted into medical centres. Comfort and nourishment will be provided to the colonists with the second wave of Grey Herons expected to arrive shortly. Joining them will be Wesley's brothers.

Rounding up his squad, Sun Tzu informs them that they have received intel on a potential location of Chinese colonists trapped in the Foundry. Knowing the bridge has been secured, Sun Tzu leads Yong Squad deeper into the occupied territory.

An abrupt drop in Maia's temperature freezes the moon. Thick snowflakes fall over the city. Ditched belongings of fleeing families, abandoned industrial vehicles, bodies caught in the violence, and other remnants of the beginning of the conflict are buried. Even their exoskeleton struggles to safeguard them against the cold. With each step, the snow crunches beneath their feet.

The silence is unnerving.

Bullet holes scar the surrounding factories and warehouses. The squad stick close to the edge of the street, moving in single file. No activity is detected. Satellite imagery shows nothing. Sun Tzu grows increasingly anxious, something that is felt by the rest of the soldiers. Each of them grip their rifle tight. Their fingers on the trigger. Wesley expected to be in the heat of a frenzied battle, not this.

"*Where have they gone?*" mumbled a soldier over the coms.

"*Keep focused,*" snapped Li, sounding just as anxious.

A flicker triggers Wesley's targeting system. Behind the collapsed scaffolding something hides. Halting the soldiers behind him, he steps out from formation. Raising his rifle, he heads over to investigate.

"*Jung,*" barked Sun Tzu.

Peering over the toppled metal platform, what he finds is utterly perplexing. Pecking at the snow is a black and white bird. It is the first creature Wesley as ever seen. The bird tilts it's head, acknowledging Wesley's presence. Totally fearless, it hops towards him, squawking loudly. Before long it spreads its wings and flies high over the warehouse.

"*Wesley,*" cried Li.

A sharp thud hits Wesley in the chest. The same place Sun Tzu stabbed him with the Jian. The impact sends a shockwave through his body. His on-screen vitals go haywire. Losing the strength in his knees, Wesley collapses to the ground.

"*Take cover,*" commanded Sun Tzu.

Yong Squad dive to safety as a barrage of bullets sweep down the street.

A visor shatters and a comrade's body falls limp. The mess is contained in their helmet. Sun Tzu watches helplessly at his two downed soldiers. This is not the same type of encounter that they experienced on the bridge. Before it was desperate. Here they are organised. Resourceful. Sun Tzu struggles to make sense of it.

With Wesley reading as only offline, he orders Li to investigate. Blindly firing back, Sun Tzu creates an opening.

Sliding along the snow, Li manages to reach his friend intact. Checking over his body, he finds a dent in the chest plate. Wesley grips Li's arm, hoarsely coughing. The two can't help but laugh with relief.

Finding cover behind the scaffolding, Wesley resets his systems. While most of the functions are restored, his vitals fail to calibrate. Looking up, his targeting system locks on to more civilians boxing them in from the other end.

"*Sir!*" called Li.

Without hesitation, Sun Tzu orders the squad to split in two. Severely outnumbered, Yong Squad entrench themselves in defensive positions. The civilian force gain ground and panic sets in. Shots are fired indiscriminately. Casualties become fatalities.

"*Control your fire,*" Sun Tzu screamed as civilian bodies fall dead.

"*We are surrounded,*" panicked a soldier as their situation intensifies. "*There are too many of them.*"

"*They are civilians,*" he said, their general doing his best to remind them.

Pulling back into cover, Wesley reloads his clip. Sparks fly as bullets ricochet off the metal platform. From above he notices a figure perched atop of the warehouse, watching the carnage. The figure pulls out a small device and holds it so that Wesley can see.

"*Get down!*"

Explosions blast through the walls of the adjacent buildings. Bricks and concrete are launched into the air, raining down onto the squad below. Sections of the building collapse, stranding the divided soldiers. A cloud of dust and snow make it impossible to see.

A gargled shriek comes from under the rubble. Wesley rushes over to find an arm sticking out from the debris. Despite his best efforts, he cannot pull this comrade free. The concrete above is dislodged, caving in around the trapped soldier.

"*Fuck!*"

The attack from the Westerners continue, making it impossible to climb over and regroup with Sun Tzu. With such low visibility, they cannot effectively fight back. The buildings either side groan as their structural integrity is compromised. It would be unwise to remain in their current position.

"*Sun Tzu? Sun Tzu?*" Li called over the coms, huddled behind the wreckage.

Wesley quickly assesses the situation. There is no time to wait on directives from their general.

"*We have to go. I will punch a hole in the enemy line. The rest of you follow,*" said Wesley, pulling Li to his feet.

"*But...*"

"*There is no time.*"

Li relays the order to what remains of the squad. Grouping together, they lay down suppressive fire as Wesley leads the charge.

Rushing at the enemy, he fires short bursts at the silhouettes that emerge from the settling dust. Mists of blood spray into the air. The odd lucky shot from the civilians fortunately bounce off his armour. Racing to the end of the street, Wesley glances back to see the others close behind.

Turing the corner, something is not quite right. The warehouse precariously begins to lean in towards their escape route. Cracks split the cement. As the structures weight shifts, Wesley knows they don't have much time until it collapses. Picking up the pace, the squad push the exoskeleton's functions as far as they can handle.

The soldier's inexperience with the full capability of the suit leads to a few mistiming their landings, tumbling into the snow. They attempt a quick recovery. The building begins to crumble and the far end comes crashing down, cutting off the civilian force. Like a wave, the rest follows. Wesley and Li watch as a few stragglers disappear under the warehouse.

Wesley's roar echoes in the streets of the Foundry. The surviving soldiers hold him back, stopping him from climbing back over. On-screen the soldier's lifelines are gone. Killed instantly.

"*Jung, we have to go. There is nothing we can do for them now,*" Li tried to reason with him.

"*Fuck!*"

With their numbers severity depleted, the Yong Squad keep to the shadows, evading the mob that pursues them. Regardless of their best efforts, the tracks they leave in the snow is an easy trail for them to follow.

Using every alleyway and path through the factories, they manage to create enough distance to lose them. Deep within the district, Li knows they are completely alone. Cutting though into an unlocked factory workshop, he orders the squad to take rest while they gather their bearings.

There is not one amongst them that does not curse their predicament. While some check their ammunition, others hope to make contact with the separated squad. Wesley rests his helmet on a workbench. Though the air in the factory is not fresh, it is crisp enough to calm his temper. The smell however is putrid.

"*This is a completely dark zone. The satellite imagery cannot find our location. It could be because of the weather, but all readings from the resistance camp are normal,*" said Li to anyone who is listening.

"*Li, look at this,*" said Wesley.

Turning to his friend, Li follows his gaze up to the ceiling. Gently swaying in the darkness are bodies hung from the metal beams. Men, women and children all with a noose around their necks. All of them Westerners.

"*What is going on here?*" remarked one of the soldiers.

"*Do you think the Chinese colonists did this?*" asked another.

"*None of this makes sense,*" said Wesley, stepping towards the centre of the room. "*That trap was too well orchestrated. The colonists had no idea we would be involved in the conflict. It was not like those explosives where set in a particularly strategical position either.*"

"*The colonists were too close to the blast, I do not think they knew about it,*" Li speculated.

"*We are being played.*"

The helmet thuds to the floor and each of the soldiers aim their sights at the workbench. The sudden noise had frightened them all. Wesley investigates, treading cautiously around the bench.

222

"Wait. Do not shoot," a nervous voice called out from behind.

Two shaking arms held in the air appear, followed by the face of a scrawny Chinese man with cracked thin rimmed spectacles. Though relieved, none of them lower their rifles.

"Do not shoot. I have a family."

"Step out slowly," ordered Li. *"What happened here?"*

"You are from Neo-Shanxi. I can tell by the dragon on your chest."

"What happened?" reiterated Wesley.

"You do not know? Why come to Maia if you do not know?" asked the man to no response. *"The CERE did not want Maia to go the way of Neo-Shanxi or Thuỷ Phủ, so they agreed to meet with representatives of the Chinese colonists to discuss concessions. But on the day, none of the CERE showed up. They and their families could not be found. Their homes where abandoned. No one was here to govern Maia. Demonstrations erupted all over the city. People began looting shops and factories. That is when the CERE and their families were found."*

"Found right here," noted Wesley, looking at the bodies above.

"Westerners blamed the Chinese. Said it was the first act of violence in a Chinese revolt on Maia," finished the man. *"Can I lower my arms now?"*

"Yes, of course," Li said apologetically. *"Do you think Chinese colonists killed these people?"*

"Who can say?" said the man, shaking his head. *"My family. I need to get back to them, otherwise they will worry."*

"Where are your family?"

"The storehouse opposite the factory. We are trying to get across the canal to Lotus Gardens, but the blockade has made it impossible."

Li rounds up his soldiers. Together they map out the quickest route back to the bridge. He draws up a contingency for if they run into the civilian force. But his plan does not sit right with everybody. Leaning against the bench Wesley stares blankly at the floor.

"Jung, we should move out," said Li.

"I am not coming."

"What are you talking about?" he asked.

Grabbing his helmet, Wesley faces the squad. *"I am going to look for Sun Tzu and the rest."*

"That is suicide," argued Li. *"If we head back to camp with the civilians, we can regather our strength and then launch a search and rescue. Sun Tzu has probably already beaten us back."*

"You cannot honestly believe that. Sun Tzu would not leave us behind," countered Wesley. *"I am not asking for anyone to join me."*

"We are with you Jung," interrupted one of his comrades.

Gradually Yong Squad begin to divide. Li watches powerlessly as his command is lost. Nothing he can say would change their minds. Wesley looks back at the two soldiers remaining by Li's side. It is a small enough unit to go undetected. Holding out his hand, Wesley wishes Li the best of luck.

"I will secure a route back to the bridge," said Li. *"Come back safe brother."*

Wesley and the squad watch as Li escorts the scrawny colonist out of the workshop. Looking back, the two give each other one last nod farewell. Placing his helmet on,

Wesley realises he has no plan, no idea of where to even begin their search, and with something jamming their signal, they are completely in the dark.

In the quiet narrow streets of the Foundry, they march through a deluge of snow. The blizzard howls and wails. They struggle against the remorseless weather, treading through the snow which now reaches the top of their shins. Power has been cut-off. There is little to guide them. Their lack of visibility is not helped by the condensation forming on the inside of their visors. Most begin to regret their decision to join Wesley, unconvinced of how much longer they can withstand the cold.

Having had no contact with Sun Tzu or the others since their separation, Wesley is surprised to receive a faint signal response. Only a few streets away, he picks up the pace.

Carried by the wind, a poetic whisper calls to Wesley.

"Little dragon. Little white dragon..."

Looking back at the squad, he is certain that no one else heard it. Pressing on, they make their way down a street with banners remaining from the demonstrations swaying in the wind. Each yellow banner has the character '*peace*' painted in black.

"Little white dragon come. This way dragon..."

The whisper calls out to him again. Like a moth drawn to a flame, Wesley follows the voice. Farther down, something else hangs from the streetlamps.

Wesley's behaviour makes the rest nervous. They tighten their grip and rest their finger firmly on the trigger. Confused quivers are shared over the coms.

"*Jung? What are you doing?*" questioned one of them.

"Little white dragon of Shanxi. Come, play at war with us..."

This time they all heard it. They head for cover, leaving Wesley exposed in the middle of the street. Calling him over, none can reach the mesmerised soldier.

He scans his surround area, trying to find the one beckoning him. A flicker in the sky triggers his targeting system. Flying high above him is the magpie. Realising they have once again stumbled into a trap, he spins around to his squad.

"*The rooftops,*" a soldier yelled.

A synchronised assault rains down upon them. Not a single shot misses its target. Rounds rip through their armour as it were made of paper. Red splatters stain the white snow. The soldiers who survive the initial onslaught fire wildly at nothing. Their systems cannot detect their attackers.

The futile resistance does not last long. Bodies lay dead in the snow, while Wesley stands unscathed.

"White Dragon, come..."

Turning his back on the massacre, Wesley heads farther down the dark street. The closer he gets to the figures swaying from the lampposts, the more they remind him of what he'd discovered hanging in the workshop. This time however, they are not colonists. Each of them wear green armour, a helmet with an orange visor and the character '*brave*' sprayed on their chests.

"Little dragon. You have found us..."

At the end of the trail of bodies, standing atop a three-story building, is a female soldier dressed in black and blue. Her auburn hair whips about in the blizzard. A bandana sits around her forehead. Flapping in the wind is a black leather half-skirt. At knife point Sun Tzu kneels, stripped naked and beaten.

"At last little white dragon, I see you. Youngest of the three sons. I see you," the woman said lyrically.

Blood trickles down Sun Tzu's wrinkled skin. Shivering in the cold, he no longer has the strength to fight back.

"*Run,*" he shouted, without looking at him.

"You are but a child playing at a game you know nothing about," she insulted. "Nothing."

The blade cuts deep. Sun Tzu jerks about as his throat is torn into. A flood of crimson fluid drains over his chest. As he chokes, a violent life of war comes to an end.

Before Wesley can act, a sniper takes their shot. The bullet tears through the back of his helmet, destroying the internal computer systems. The force of the impact knocks Wesley unconscious.

A loud piercing screech rings in his ears. Wesley opens his eyes to distorted flashing images. Feeling nauseous, he removes his helmet to find it soaked with blood from a cut at the back of his head. Wesley imagines that he has only been out for a minute or two.

Couching in front of him is the redheaded woman. Her skin is a tapestry of combat and age. The letters 'S.E.L.' are engraved into her breastplate. Around her arm is a band with an emblem of a magpie. She studies him with the same mannerisms as the bird. Reaching for his rifle, he finds it has already been seized. As he stands, she mimics.

Magpie smiles with open arms. "Here I am. Nothing stands between me and you, little dragon."

Muffled cries come from the nearby storehouse. Women and children plea for help. Magpie watches his indecisive reactions. Taking a step forward, she takes one step backwards.

Again, the cries call out. Wesley turns his attention to the building. The open doorway leads to a pitch-black corridor. It is most certainly a trap, but the colonists' screams play on his conscience. Submitting to her game, Wesley races into the storehouse.

In the darkness, he follows the calls. He runs his hand along the concrete wall to guide himself, memorising the path to the exit just in case. A strong whiff of chemicals leaves him lightheaded.

To maintain his focus, Wesley recites Yong Squads five rules: *You let one down, you let all down; Individuals die, units survive; Broken windows lead to broken limbs; Sun Tzu is absolute; Chinese we are, Chinese we will stay*.

Never has Wesley felt so alone. Those who chose to join him only wound up dead. Never has he felt so venerable. His helmet shattered beyond use and nothing to defend himself with. The Neo-Shanxi Army's General is dead. There is no longer anyone in charge of this operation. And finally, the CERE bodies decorating the ceiling of the workshop. As much as Shanxi has been played, so too have the people of Maia. Ethnicity was the powder keg that ignited this whole revolt, yet no one seems to know why they are fighting. How foolish have they all been.

Finding a closed door with a dim light shining though the bottom, Wesley cautiously enters. The rusty hinges, something he has never experienced before, shriek as the door opens. In the centre of the room he finds Chinese colonists tied to barrels. Though they are all blindfolded, they turn to face him.

"*Help us, please,*" one of them sobbed.

"*I will get you out,*" Wesley reassured them.

Without a knife or anything sharp laying around in the room, the restraints are near on impossible to undo. Realising that fiddling about with the knots is not doing anything to help, he looks around for another way to free them. Peering behind one of the captives, Wesley finds a small detonator blinking red. Not having pieced it together until this very moment, the smell of chemicals is coming from the barrels. With little time left, Wesley makes a run for it.

"*Wait!*" screamed the colonists. "*Where are you going?*"

A bright white light blisters through concrete, engulfing the whole building. The intense heat melts all it can.

Any material left is scorched by the chemical compound, fizzling away. The air becomes toxic. Charred pieces of the colonists remain, none of which could be said to resemble anything human.

Flaying out onto the street, Wesley squeals as the chemical splash corrodes the skin down the right side of his face. It does not take long for the chemical to eat its way through his exoskeleton, burning his neck and chest. To smother the pain, he buries himself into the snow. His throat swells and he beings to suffocate.

"*He is awake. Get the doctor,*" instructed a familiar voice.

"*Wesley, do not move. Stay right where you are, someone is coming to help,*" said another familiar voice.

Mustering the will to open his eyes, Wesley finds himself in a makeshift infirmary. Dressing covers half his face, while his neck and chest are wrapped in bandages. Lodged down his larynx is a tube feeding him oxygen. The anaesthetic does little to negate the immense discomfort he is experiencing. His brothers wait by his bedside as someone fetches assistance.

Attempting to speak, Wesley gags, then coughs in agony.

"*The doctor said you should not talk,*" said Alistair.

Moving his arm, Wesley does not get far before realising he is attached to an IV. Pulling at the tubes, he raises his hand to inspect his injuries. He cannot feel a thing.

"*Do not touch,*" cautioned Alistair, placing his brother's arm back down to his side.

"*The doctor will be here soon. Just lay still,*" said Oscar, peering out into the hallway.

Having regained some clarity in his thoughts, Wesley is desperate to be given an update on everything that has happened since he fell asleep. Gesturing to his brothers, he hopes they understand.

"*The time?*" Alistair asked confused.

"*You have been out for a day, pretty much twenty-four hours. Or at least since they found you,*" explained Oscar, realising what his brother was asking.

"The soldiers who rescued the family from the Foundry went straight back out to look for you. You are the only survivor," continued Alistair, then his tone changed, "no one else has managed to come back from the central district. There is no communication. All our satellite imagery shows no activity, yet the colonists tell us that is where the worst of the fighting is. No one knows what is going on."

Tears run down Wesley's cheek. Trying to hold back his emotions in fear of the physical pain it will cause him, he fails to do so.

"I am sorry brother."

At that moment, the doctor bursts into the room, barging past Oscar. Flipping through Wesley's readings on his tablet, he peers over his glasses at the young soldier. Quietly contemplating, the brothers wait for the news.

"I thought I told you two not to excite him?" scolded the doctor. "Mr Jung, I will be honest, how you survived is beyond any of the staff here. You have suffered third degree burns to your face, neck and chest. We have cleaned your wounds and cut away some of the tissue to ensure it is clear of chemicals. There is still some material from your suit fused to your skin. Of course, this means there is a danger that it may contain some chemical residue, so we shall extract it when you have had time to rest. Proper treatment, in terms of skin grafts, will have to wait until we return to Shanxi. We will do the best we can for you."

"Thank you, Doctor," said Oscar.

"The chemical you were exposed to blistered your windpipe. I can give you something for the pain, but speaking and swallowing may be unpleasant for months to come. In the meantime, we will feed you fluids and oxygen through tubes," explained the doctor, then he paused. "*It was amazing that they found you when they did.*"

Tapping the dressing on his face, Wesley wants to see for himself.

"*I strongly advise against that Mr Jung.*"

Watching his brother become distressed, Oscar intervenes. "*Show him.*"

Finding a mirror from the nearby dresser, Alistair holds it out in front of Wesley. The doctor carefully pulls away the dressing, his hands shaking all the while. With it completely removed, Wesley stares long and hard at his reflection.

Where his dragon once was, white stiff leathery skin disfigures his hansom face. It looks as though his skin has fused with his teeth. Very little covers the jawbone. With a small nod, the doctor redresses the wound and leaves the brothers in peace.

"*It looks bad now, but when we return home they will have you back to the way you were,*" Oscar attempted to comfort him. "*Much more of this and we will need to withdraw.*"

"*That is out of the question,*" said Alistair.

Closing the door, Oscar does not wish to disrupt the rest of the floor. Hanging his head, he is just about to speak when Alistair interrupts.

"*We are not leaving those people trapped in the central district.*"

"*Alistair, we are not fighting some crusade. We were supposed to restore stability to the colony, yet casualties have far exceeded expectation. Both in civilian and our forces. Our own brother amongst them. It is reasonable to accept that we have done all that we can. Call the* evacuation and bring the colonist in the resistance camp back to Shanxi with us."

"Grandfather trusted us to bring peace to Maia," countered Alistair.

"And, where is he? Home, safe. Do not let Grandfather move us like pawns."

"If we cannot quell a civilian force, what chance do you think Shanxi will have against the full might of the CERE?" Alistair explained the full extent of their colony's transgression. "This has never been about Maia. It is about our future. If we leave now, Shanxi will show it is weak."

Having listened to his brothers bicker for long enough, Wesley goes to speak, forgetting about the tubes in his throat. The pain leaves him squirming about in bed. Both brothers rush to his care, Oscar administers some pain relief by the simple press of a button. They wait for him to relax.

"Do not move. Lay back and get some sleep," insisted Alistair.

Oscar tries one last time to convince his brother. "There will be no army to defend Shanxi if we stay here. The CERE will not see us as weak, but just. Peacekeepers in a conflict too far for them to mediate themselves. If you cannot do this for our people, then do it for our brother."

The medication has made Wesley too drowsy for him to protest. His anger subsides to pity. Then pity into shame. Laying there powerless, his eyelids become heavy. Before he drifts off to sleep he hears the end of his brothers' argument.

"Our army will have until sunrise. We will launch one last expedition to save as many colonists from the Foundry as possible. Then we will evacuate."

"Thank you, brother…"

A loud splutter from the next room wakes Wesley. Unsure of how long he has been asleep, the fact it is still dark means there is still time. There is no way Wesley is leaving Maia with her alive.

He pulls the IV drips from his arm. Tilting his head back as far as it will go, he tugs the tubes out from his throat. His insides feel raw, gagging and choking as the last few inches are removed. Each short sharp breath of Maia's cold air is punishing. Almost regretting his actions, Wesley looks at the tubes and forgoes reinserting them.

Sneaking along next door, he finds a small ward with the injured sprawled across the floor. Many of these men have only received basic treatment to keep them alive, a result of the unexpected workload that the medical staff are trying to keep up with. Most of their wounds need redressing. Others desperately need their next dosage of pain relief. Resting in one of the only beds is the Westerner who refused Wesley's help at the bridge.

"What do you want?" the Westerner disgruntledly questioned in his best English.

Leaning in close, Wesley fights to get each of his words out. "Know...happened...workshop. Not...Chinese. Dark...Zone, who?"

"You saw?" uttered the man. "No one knows who they are. No one comes back alive. They gave the colonists weapons, then they went to war against them."

"Why...kill...Chinese?"

Sheepishly the Westerner averts his gaze, he cannot fathom an answer. Wesley begins to understand the fear that has gripped this planet. Leaving the man to his own guilt, Wesley searches for some armour.

The generals relay Alistair's orders and the battle along the canal intensifies. The wounded are dragged through the camp. Soldiers ferry crates of ammunition to the frontline. Others prepare the Grey Herons for the evacuation. Without a squad, Li has been assigned to such menial tasks.

From the shadows, Wesley calls him over away from the watchful eyes of their superiors.

Taking one look at him, Li knows he has snuck out. *"What are you doing here? You need to be resting."*

"Squad...dead," Wesley informed him.

"I know, Sun Tzu too. Their bodies are still out there," Li admitted.

"Soldiers...Foundry."

"You mean the CERE have forces on Maia?"

Wesley shakes his head. "S...E...L."

"S.E.L.?" questioned Li. *"We have been given the order to withdraw."*

"Cannot...leave...unfinished," said Wesley. *"Come..."*

Taking a deep breath, Li contemplates the dangers they would be walking into. They would have no backup, confronting an unknown enemy that slaughtered their comrades. Executed their leader. Destroyed the family Li had found. It is anger that drives him. The same anger driving Wesley.

"For Yong Squad," he said with a steely look of determination.

*

235

Passed the fighting along the canal, Li and Wesley return to the silent narrow streets that weave in and about the concrete factories and warehouses. To avoid detection, they have both ditched their helmets. Following the route Li used to find Wesley, their old tracks have been erased by the snow and the blood from the massacre buried.

The bodies hanging from the lampposts tell them that they are heading in the right direction. This time however, the whole street is adorned with bodies. Colonists, Western and Chinese, and Shanxi soldiers dangle above the blanketed ground. Their skin turned shades of blue and purple. Icicles drip from their fingertips.

Outside the ruins of the storehouse, Sun Tzu is displayed, suspended from his ankles. Naked and maimed, he has been bled like an animal.

Venturing blindly farther into the Foundry, the occasional burst of gunfire is their only clue of S.E.L.'s whereabouts. Craters scar the grey concrete structures. Red shadows reveal the nature of executions. Frozen under the snow lay their victims. Men, women and children, the killing is indiscriminate.

Stamping her foot down into the chest of a civilian, Magpie pins him in place. Unconcerned with his begging, her mannerisms once again imitate that of the bird's. Pressing the muzzle of her pistol against his forehead, his begging turns into blubbering. She squeezed the trigger.

Fragments of bone and brain splatter the wall. She lifts her foot and the corpse rolls into the snow. Surrounded by those in her command, Magpie basks in the butchery.

Out from the darkness, Wesley stands alone before the soldiers of black and blue. They find his presence amusing, but none as much as their auburn-haired leader.

"Little white dragon, you are tougher than I gave you credit," she said. Stepping forward to greet him, she signals for her squad to stay put. "Still you have learnt nothing. The gift of a second life was bestowed upon you, yet you come crawling back into the frays of death, relinquishing yourself of such mercy."

Magpie raises her pistol, yet he does not falter. A quick glance over at the alleyway is enough to give away his plan. But it is too late. Before she can warn her men, Li jumps out from behind cover and aims the grenade launcher at the distracted group of soldiers. Her squad are blown limb from limb.

Spinning back around, Magpie too is caught off guard. Giving her no chance to retaliate, Wesley aims his shot and fires. She lands with her face in the bloodied snow.

Li steps over the bodies, confirming the kills. The lenses of the masks are cracked. On each of their armbands, they each wear emblems of beasts, insects and birds that neither of the Neo-Shanxi boys recognise. There is one body they leave until last. Her hair fluttering in the blizzard.

Above them, the squawking bird rests on a ledge, watching as ever.

Jabbing the body with the butt of his *Dragon Crescent*, Wesley is confident enough to examine closer. To his surprise, she rolls overs easily. Caught in the breast plate is the bullet. Her eyes open, fixed on Wesley.

Wild and mad, she moves in ways Wesley thought not possible. Wrestling him to the ground, her legs wrap around him and she relieves him of his rifle.

Li rushes into to help, but Magpie takes her knife and embeds it into his leg. Yanking at the blade, it tears through the microfibers of his exoskeleton. Finding her pistol on the ground, she unloads round after round at him. The force of the barrage of bullets sends Li hurtling backwards.

Squirming out of her clutches, Wesley wheezes as he catches his breath. A poorly aimed shot bounces off his shoulder pad. The pistol clicks as she frantically pulls the trigger again. Giving her no time to reload, he pounces, only to be thrown back to the ground. Rushing at him with a kick, Magpie buys enough time to make a run for the nearest factory.

Li manages to let off a few shots before she completely vanishes.

"*Jung,*" Li called out in pain. "*I am alright. Go get her. I will be right behind you.*"

Reaching high into the factory are several industrial sized cisterns. Scaffolding and suspended walkways ascend to the top. Chains rattle like wind chimes.

The stale metallic taste of the air aggravates Wesley's throat. Coughing, he steadies himself against a steel pillar. In the little light there is, droplets of blood glisten, leaving a trail to follow. Li must have hit her.

Footsteps clang against metal as she runs overhead. Firing up into the levels above, sparks fly, hitting nothing.

Magpie laughs.

"Come, White Dragon. I promise you death."

With an unwavering resolve, Wesley begins the chase. Keeping his steps light, the trail of blood leads the way.

Along the pathway between two cisterns, Wesley realises how open he has left himself. Vigilantly he watches any potential hiding spots. Twitching at the slightest of noises. Anticipating any disturbances felt in the air.

Swinging out from cover, Magpie darts for the stairs as they exchange fire. Twangs echo as metal collides with metal. Wesley manages to reach safety behind some machinery. Already he knows she managed to escape again.

Surprising him from above, he is only just able to jump out of the way of bullets raining down. From the railing, she watches him with a manic look, as if she was enjoying their battle.

Nowhere else to run to but the roof, Magpie holds off her pursuer as far back as her aim will allow. Wounded while escaping into the factory, the climb has exasperated blood loss. Pale and faint, her vision blurs. Loading the final clip, she breaks for the last place she has left to go.

Wesley notices the gas pipes running down the side of the tank next to him. While he dislodges a pipe with his rifle, he calls Li over the coms.

"I am here Jung. I do not think I will be able to get to you up there."

"On...signal...grenade...top...floor."

"You want me to grenade the top floor of the factory?" Li clarified, receiving a grunt in response.

The view from the rooftop is obscured by the blizzard. A few orange glows can be made out from distant fires, but nothing else. Magpie stands waiting for him. One hand placing pressure on her side, the other pointing her pistol. Neither of them make any sudden moves.

"Show me," demanded Magpie. "Show me your true self."

Dropping his weapon, Wesley tears the dressing from his face, exposing the leathery skin fused to his teeth. She almost mistakes him for smiling.

Her whisper is carried by the wind. "I see you."

"I...see...you," wheezed Wesley.

Madly the auburn-haired soldier begins to laugh. In her hysterics, she does not hear Wesley callout to Li. Just as instructed, Li launches a grenade through the top window. The explosion ignites the gas, blowing away the front of the building.

The dust settles and Wesley finds himself on what remains of the rooftop. The air scratches his throat, so he does his best not to inhale large breaths. A ringing in his ears muffles the world around him. Yet he can still hear her laughter.

Where she was standing is a gaping hole in the side of the factory. Cautiously he scales down the rubble to find her. Impaled on steel rods, she watches as Wesley approaches. Even now, he is careful not to get too close.

"Little dragon, I am impressed," she sputtered.

"Why...all...this...murder?" he asked, half not expecting to receive an answer.

"Terror to prevent terror. I am committed to the contradiction," she said, smiling to Wesley's bemusement. "Red and gold. He saw it too...red and gold."

"Who...?" Wesley asked.

"Wolf," she answered to another blank look. "The soldier responsible for ending the war. The man who has prevented countless others from erupting. Wolf did what was necessary to protect peace. His only failing was to save a little girl from the mountains of China."

"Little...girl?"

"Zhang Li," she coughed, growing weak.

While Wesley struggles to understand the connection between his mother and this group, Magpie pulls out a warn leather diary from her pocket. She places it into his hands.

"It is your turn now, White Dragon. Do you have the resolve to do what is necessary? To prevent terror and bring about peace? Are you committed? I have done what I set out to do, it is your turn."

"You...lost," said Wesley, undermining her sense of triumph.

She sputters a laugh. "Foolish dragon. I have done exactly what I came here to do. Are you truly so blind? S.E.L. came to Maia, the Neo-Shanxi Army was drawn from Delta Nine. Neo-Shanxi has fallen..."

Magpie's last words leave Wesley feeling sick. Falling into the rubble, he watches as her life fades away. In death, she finds her peace.

Watching them are ghostly figures of black and blue. As Li's calls come closer, the figures disappear into the snowy streets. Wesley grips the diary tightly in his hands. His victory snuffed out and replaced by a deep dread.

*

As Maia orbits Thule, the sun breaks over the colony. The planet begins to warm and the frozen surface melts. Travelling down the mountains, rivers feed the great shimmering seas of Maia. In the city, the water trickles off the roofs, finding its way into the canals.

In only his underwear, Wesley watches from the window as the whole planet is transformed.

241

A knock on the door disturbs Wesley's exhausted daze. Oscar enters the room carrying a cup of tea. Though he knows the beverage is not for him, it would be a welcome remedy if he were able to swallow. The brothers stand side by side admiring the view.

"*Can hardly believe this is the same planet,*" said Oscar. Fully appreciating that Wesley cannot make small talk in his current state, he relays the message he was given by the doctor. "*The nurse will be here soon to clean up your wounds and give you a change of clothes. Breakfast was mentioned, but the manner which you will be fed, do not get too excited.*"

Wesley sniggers, then coughs.

"*Your friend is in the next room by the way,*" Oscar informed him, then gently blows to cool his drink. "*What you two did was reckless and foolish, but everyone here on Maia is in your debt. Shortly after you returned to camp, Thuỷ Phủ forces managed to push through. They reported no major resistance in the Foundry.*"

"S...E...L...?" asked Wesley.

"*A team was sent to the coordinates Li gave, but no bodies were recovered,*" he explained. "*I cannot believe the CERE had a military presence on Maia.*"

Wesley wishes that he could explain, but it is as futile as much as he does not have the capability to do so. Instead he changes the subject to their brother.

"*Alistair? You have played your role as a soldier, now he gets to play his as a politician. As we speak he is sitting through meeting after meeting, striking an accord with both Western and Chinese colonists. It all sounds incredibly dull if you ask me,*" jested Oscar.

"*Why...you...Maia?*"

He smiles. *"I am the bargaining chip. Proof that an alliance with Neo-Shanxi would be mutually beneficial. Once all the talks are over, I will get to work on improving the TFP and the colony's facilities."*

Turning their attention back to the window, they watch as children play outside in the pavilion. So much of the Lotus Gardens is reminiscent of home. Far out along the horizon, dark clouds gather. The colony will only have a few hours of good weather before the storm hits.

On the bedside cabinet, the warn diary lays unopened. Intrigued by the souvenir his brother came back with, Oscar inspects the tatty old thing. Careful not to ruin the pages, he quickly flicks through. The first third of the diary is written in English, the second in two languages he cannot read and the final third is blank. Turning back to the first page, he deciphers the scruffy handwriting.

"'All warfare is based on deception. Hence, when we are able to attack, we must seem unable; when using our forces, we must appear inactive; when we are near, we must make the enemy believe we are far away; when far away, we must make them believe we are near...'

"A quote from Sun Tzu, how very ominous," he joked, not realising the look on Wesley's face. *"I am sorry brother. None of this should have ever of happened. Your squad. I cannot imagine the pain you are going through right now. Anything that you need, just ask."*

Unable to prevent his emotional outpour, Wesley breaks down into tears. Oscar places his tea on the cabinet and consoles his younger brother. Burring his head into Oscar's shoulder, the discomfort of crying aggravates his throat. There is little either of them can do to ease the pain.

Outside, Wesley notices the contrails that mark the sky. Wiping away the tears, he tracks the vessels descending into Maia's atmosphere. As more follow, the colony's sirens begin to wail. Landing just outside the district are Grey Herons from Shanxi.

Charging through the infirmary, Wesley manages to find some trousers before joining the rest of the staff heading towards the landing field. Confused speculation disperses amongst the congregating crowds. Medics and soldiers prepare themselves for the worst.

A scuffed and dented Grey Heron lands at the edge of the Lotus Gardens. Wesley and Oscar wait anxiously. The hatch swings open and a frightened, blood-soaked colonist stumbles out.

"Help! We need help!"

Without hesitation Oscar springs into action. Climbing on board, he begins to help carry the injured out of the boat. People rush towards the Grey Herons pulling survivors out into the city.

Radio contact is made with Shanxi and Thuỷ Phủ soldiers demanding assistance. A few hope to break up the meeting Alistair is currently attending.

Maia is once again plunged into chaos. All around him, Shanxi colonists are being wrapped in blankets, given water, carried off on stretchers or laid out in rows. Mothers search for their children. Lone men stroll aimlessly with a sombre detachment, having already witnessed the loss of loved ones. Boat after boat, the story is the same.

Seeking answers, Wesley tries anybody willing to talk. An old man, with his head in bloody bandages and the Neo-Shanxi Dragon on his jacket, recognises him.

"Du Jianguo and the CERE sympathisers escaped. They stormed the Assembly with CERE soldiers and shot anyone in support of the Chairman. Zhang has been charged with treason and your family...they have all been detained. No one knows what has happened to them," the old man explained.

"Black...blue...?" asked Wesley.

"Yes. How did you?" said the man surprised.

Before he can expect an answer, Wesley drifts off farther into the massing refugees. The cold muddy earth beneath his bare feet has turned to slush. Those trying to offer aid slip and slide, causing more disorder.

"Someone! He is dying," a voice cried out.

Navigating through the crowd, Wesley finds a young woman nursing his father in her lap. Charles looks pale, covered in blood and mud. Begging for anyone to help, she no longer has the strength to carry him. As he kneels beside her, she finds his appearance unsettling.

"Please, you have to help him."

A reassuring nod is all he can give her. Taking his father in his arms, Wesley marches towards the nearest available doctor. He is shocked at how feeble Charles feels.

Panicking, Wesley forgets to look where he is walking and trips over a small child, the two of them come crashing down into the mud. Amongst the chaos, nobody even notices their tumble. Wheezing as he claws his way over to his father's body, Wesley slowly comes to an acceptance.

He places an ear against Charles' lips, there is no sign of life. Holding his father tight, he waits for someone to find them.

The storm eventually came. Maia and Shanxi colonists buried their families by a lake north of the city. Hundreds of graves litter the field. Mass ceremonies were offered, most chose to keep the affair private. Kind-hearted volunteers laid to rest those who have no one left to perform the service for them. Though there wasn't much organisation in the layout, people found the compassion to allow enough space for loved ones to join them later. The bodies of soldiers who died during the revolt are to be cremated in the days to come, returned home when possible. Such uncertainty hangs in the air.

Every family was given a red column, excess material found in one of the storehouses, a brush and black paint. Charles was no exception. Wesley feeds the column into the ground. Oscar and Alistair fill the gaps. In English, his full name and title is written. Nothing else.

The three sons stand before their father's tombstone, drenched, muddy and emotionally drained. None of them can properly grieve. All that has happened is eclipsed by the fear of what is happening on Shanxi and to their families. Those fears go unspoken in case the worst is true.

"We should say something," Oscar muttered in English. He picks up the bottle of whiskey held upright by the mud and takes a large swig. "To a man who gave humanity the stars."

"To a father who sacrificed everything for his children," Alistair continued, taking a drink.

"Father…" Wesley attempted.

Giving up, he is passed the bottle and lets the liquid trickle down his throat. Instantly he coughs it up.

Finally, they pour one last measure as an offering to their father.

Quietly they stand. All around them people morn. The drivels of grief begin to irritate the three sons. Growing restless, Wesley is the first to make the move to leave.

"Brother wait," interrupted Alistair. "I have something for you. It seems ridiculous now, but still."

"Keep...it..." Wesley scoffed.

"We will find the strength to overcome this, as long as we are together," said his brother.

Holding out his hand, Alistair gifts him a ring made of the finest Shanxi silver. Inscribed on the outside is the character '*family*'. Oscar also receives one.

"'*You must defend your honour and your family*'," Oscar inspected the inside. "Thank you, brother."

Surprised to find it a perfect fit, Wesley offers a crooked smile in appreciation. Leading the way back to the city, the brothers will allow themselves one drunken night of grief before strategizing how they intend to save their families.

Neo-Shanxi

Li Jung

A gentle breeze brushes Li's cheek. Regaining consciousness, her vision takes a while to adjust to the blackness she finds herself in. Her wrists are bound behind her back. Wire cuts into her ankles that are tied to the legs of the chair. She gasps quietly, not wanting to alert her captor. The stench in the air is something awful. Damp and festering.

An inhuman growl mummers in the darkness. Patters of paws circle her. Two pairs of dark beady eyes hungrily glare.

Directly in front, another pair watch her. But these are large, bug like eyes. The figure lets out a muffled gratified moan. Striking a flare, the red glow reveals the soldier. The uniform is similar to the woman's who threatened her and her baby in New York all those years ago. On his armband is an image of two dogs, just like the creatures that join him at his feet.

The flare is thrown to the floor.

"It is so nice to see that you came dressed in your finest," mocked Dogs.

Surrounding them are the surviving works of Li Hu's depiction of Nanjing, hung against a jade backdrop. With her own work on display here, Li recognises she is in the Shanxi Gallery of the Assembly building.

"We have been following you and your husband's career closely for quite some time. What a shame that such brilliance was wasted on an undeserving people."

Startled by the vicious barking of the dogs, Li begins to hyperventilate. All three creatures can smell her fear. Excited by it. She watches her reflection in the lenses as the soldier creeps towards her.

Drawing his knife, he runs the blade along her leg, careful not to break the skin. In one flick, the seam of her cheongsam is undone to her hip. Li pleads with the soldier.

"I am not interested in your flesh," said Dogs, cutting her free from the bonds.

Li sits trembling, rubbing her swore wrists better. As if it were merely a child's game, Dogs finds out a small sand timer and begins the countdown.

"I cannot say the same for them."

The creatures' barking becomes incessant. Drool dangles from their fangs. They have been starved specially for this occasion.

Shoving the soldier to the floor, Li uses all the energy she has left to flee. Realising she won't make it far wearing heels, she kicks them off, leaving them behind. Though she has visited the gallery many times, all the exhibits look the same in the dark. Trying to find a point of reference, she knocks priceless works of art off the walls. The racket echoes through the gallery.

Banging on locked doors and disabled elevators, Li knows she has not got much time left until the dogs catch her. Her pace is impaired by her distress. Hopelessly looking around, a gentle breeze touches her skin. It is cool and calming, calling to her.

Following the flow of air to a shattered window, shards of glass carpet the floor. Any reservations Li had are forgotten as the howls of the beasts draw near. No matter how lightly she treads, glass pierces her skin. Bloody footprints make their way to the ledge.

Overlooking the colony, Li clings onto the vermillion curtain. Across the canyon, the TFP stands proud.

The fear withers and is replaced by fond memories filled with love and joy. Charles offering her a seat next to him during their first lecture at university; the first step she took onto Delta Nine soil; nights spent lying in bed with Charles as they listened to the terraforming atmosphere; holding each one of her sons in her arms for the first time; watching them as they played in the Imperial Gardens; becoming a grandmother to three beautiful children. Her life had been a good one, she smiled.

Li lets go of the curtain.

POST-TERRA FIRMA

THREE SONS

COMING SOON

24910329R00158

Printed in Great Britain
by Amazon